Secret Rooms and Stolen Kisses

By:

Brooke St. James

No part of this book may be used or reproduced in any form or by any means without prior written permission of the author.

Other titles available from Brooke St. James:

Another Shot:
(A Modern-Day Ruth and Boaz Story)

When Lightning Strikes

Something of a Storm (All in Good Time #1)
Someone Someday (All in Good Time #2)

Finally My Forever (Meant for Me #1)
Finally My Heart's Desire (Meant for Me #2)
Finally My Happy Ending (Meant for Me #3)

Shot by Cupid's Arrow

Dreams of Us

Meet Me in Myrtle Beach (Hunt Family #1)
Kiss Me in Carolina (Hunt Family #2)
California's Calling (Hunt Family #3)
Back to the Beach (Hunt Family #4)
It's About Time (Hunt Family #5)

Loved Bayou (Martin Family #1)
Dear California (Martin Family #2)
My One Regret (Martin Family #3)
Broken and Beautiful (Martin Family #4)
Back to the Bayou (Martin Family #5)

Almost Christmas

JFK to Dublin (Shower & Shelter Artist Collective #1)
Not Your Average Joe (Shower & Shelter Artist Collective #2)
So Much for Boundaries (Shower & Shelter Artist Collective #3)
Suddenly Starstruck (Shower & Shelter Artist Collective #4)
Love Stung (Shower & Shelter Artist Collective #5)
My American Angel (Shower & Shelter Artist Collective #6)

Summer of '65 (Bishop Family #1)
Jesse's Girl (Bishop Family #2)
Maybe Memphis (Bishop Family #3)
So Happy Together (Bishop Family #4)
My Little Gypsy (Bishop Family #5)
Malibu by Moonlight (Bishop Family #6)
The Harder They Fall (Bishop Family #7)
Come Friday (Bishop Family #8)
Something Lovely (Bishop Family #9)

3

So This is Love (Miami Stories #1)
All In (Miami Stories #2)
Something Precious (Miami Stories #3)

The Suite Life (The Family Stone #1)
Feels Like Forever (The Family Stone #2)
Treat You Better (The Family Stone #3)
The Sweetheart of Summer Street (The Family Stone #4)
Out of Nowhere (The Family Stone #5)

Delicate Balance (The Blair Brothers #1)
Cherished (The Blair Brothers #2)
The Whole Story (The Blair Brothers #3)
Dream Chaser (Blair Brothers #4)

Kiss & Tell (Novella) (Tanner Family #0)
Mischief & Mayhem (Tanner Family #1)
Reckless & Wild (Tanner Family #2)
Heart & Soul (Tanner Family #3)
Me & Mister Everything (Tanner Family #4)
Through & Through (Tanner Family #5)
Lost & Found (Tanner Family #6)
Sparks & Embers (Tanner Family #7)
Young & Wild (Tanner Family #8)

Easy Does It (Bank Street Stories #1)
The Trouble with Crushes (Bank Street Stories #2)
A King for Christmas (A Bank Street Christmas)
Diamonds Are Forever (Bank Street Stories #3)
Secret Rooms and Stolen Kisses (Bank Street Stories #4)

4

Chapter 1

Galveston Island, Texas
Spring, 1992
Tara Castro
(Tess & Billy's firstborn)

I walked into Carson's Diner feeling confident and happy. I knew I would get more and more nervous during the next hour as my meeting drew closer. But for now, I felt great. I had done a lot of preparation for this day. I knew what I was going to say, and I had predicted how it would go.

"Girl, you are in la-la land," Jesse said, as I sat down opposite her in the booth.

It was busy in Carson's Diner, or she would have stood and hugged me. Jesse was one of my best friends from high school. She was off at college now, but she was in town for the weekend, and I was meeting her for lunch before she headed back.

She looked at me with a comical smirk, like she was wondering why I was so distracted. "I was waving and trying to get your attention the whole time—ever since you walked in."

I smiled as I got settled in my seat. "I knew you would be at this booth, so I just headed this way without even looking at where I was going."

"No kidding," she said. "You looked like you were on another planet. You look good. Where are you going? Why are you all dressed up?"

"That meeting, remember? That's why I was spacing out. I was thinking about what I'll say."

I glanced all around, scanning the table and noticing that Jesse had already ordered my drink—a soda, presumably diet, with a lime, just how I loved it. She always remembered.

"What's the meeting all about?" Jesse asked. "It sounds so businesslike to say you're going to a meeting."

"It *is* businesslike," I said. "I set up the meeting through a woman who wasn't even my landlord—his secretary, I think."

"And you're trying to rent the jewelry store that's downstairs from your apartment?"

"Yes," I said. "It's not open anymore, though. Now that Mister McCain retired, it'll just be empty until someone else rents it, and I can't see any reason why that someone shouldn't be me."

"Of course, it'll be you," Jesse said confidently, even though she had been away at college and didn't know the details of my plan.

"Yep," I agreed.

"I wonder how much a place like that would cost to rent," she said.

"I know for sure how much it'll cost," I said. "Eight hundred dollars."

"Eight hundred dollars?" she asked in disbelief. "A *month*?"

"That's actually a really great deal," I said, but I quickly turned to our waitress who had just walked up. "Hey, Maggie," I said since she was now standing beside our table.

"Hey there, Tara, what can I getcha today?"

"A burger, please."

"Fries or mashed potatoes?" She asked because she knew I switched it up between those two.

"Mashed potatoes."

"With brown gravy," she said as a statement and not a question as she wrote it down for the cook. I smiled at her for knowing my order.

"And you, Jesse?"

"I just want some french fries, please." Jesse handed Maggie her menu. "Large. And the chili cheese ones, please. With jalapenos… and grilled mushrooms. You can put those on top. And maybe a little bacon, too, if you don't mind."

"Okay, so, chili cheese fries with peppers, mushrooms, and bacon," Maggie said, confirming. "Did you say onions, too?"

"No onions," Jesse said. "But I do want all the other stuff."

Maggie smiled and shook her head at Jesse as she walked away. Jesse looked at me and shrugged. She was not at all ashamed about wanting some of everything on her fries.

"Seriously, some fried shrimp would be good on those, too," Jesse said. "I'm not going to ask her now that she's walking off, but some of that popcorn fried shrimp would be so good with that. I should have probably asked for shrimp instead of bacon."

I made a face when I imagined shrimp on top of all that other stuff. But this sort of order was nothing new for me. Jesse and I had been friends since eighth grade. I was used to her eating weird combinations of things. If there was a restaurant that served one bite of everything on one plate, Jesse would order it. She was always asking for extra stuff or a side of this or that. That girl loved to eat. You would never know it looking at her, though. She had always been long and lean and thin-framed—not at all like me. I really had to watch what I ate in order to maintain a certain figure.

I had to do this for ballet, which was a passion of mine. It may seem odd for a ballerina to order a burger and mashed potatoes with gravy in the first place, but eating salads wasn't the way I dieted. I was the type who ate whatever I wanted but only allowed myself small portions of it. Today, I would eat half of the burger and a few bites of the potatoes and take the rest of it home with me to eat for dinner tonight.

Both Jesse and I were dancers, and Jesse never had to diet for a recital or worry about what she ate at all. It didn't surprise me that she ordered all that stuff on her fries, and I had no doubt that she would eat most or all of it.

"So, is it the owner of the building you're meeting? Or the property manager?" she asked, glancing at me as she spread butter on a cracker.

"Yeah, no. He's my landlord. I *think* it's the landlord, at least. That was what the lady said. I don't even know the guy. I pay rent to him every month, and I've never even met him. He doesn't live here. He's Mrs. Harper's son. He inherited the building when Mrs. Harper passed away. You remember her."

"Hmm," Jesse made a noise like she was trying to seem interested.

"He lives out of state," I continued. "I mail the rent to Nashville."

"Nashville, Tennessee?" Jesse asked, sounding surprised.

"No, Nashville, Alabama," I said, teasing her. I smiled and added, "Yes, Nashville, Tennessee. Brentwood. It's near Nashville. I looked it up."

"How is he your landlord if he doesn't even live here? What if you need something fixed?"

I shrugged. "I rarely do," I said. "But there is a guy who comes by sometimes. He fixed my light switch. I had to call the secretary for that, too."

Jesse shook her head, looking confused and still chewing. "I don't even know this Mrs. Harper lady you're talking about," she said.

"The lady who used to live in my apartment years ago, remember? You remember her from when we were in high school," I said.

Mrs. Harper had passed a while back. Jesse made a face like she was trying to remember, but I could tell she had no clue.

"She was the lady who used to sit at the window and yell down at people," I said.

"Oh, my goodness. Seriously? The one who told Derek Singleton to put his shirt on or she was calling the cops?"

"Yes," I said, laughing at the memory as I took a sip of my soda. "And the one who called Kevin Martin's dad and told him he was driving too fast down Bank Street every day."

"Oh, that's when he was working here, huh?" she said, talking about the diner.

I nodded.

"That's the same lady you're talking about? I didn't know she owned the building."

"No one did," I said. "Not until she died. My mom rented one of those upstairs apartments when she first moved to Galveston. She and dad lived next to Mrs. Harper for years, they were in 203. And they had no idea she owned the building. My parents said they mailed the rent to a post office box. Mister McCain ran that jewelry store with Joan Harper living right upstairs, and *he* never even knew she was his landlord. He didn't know until she died and her son took over the place."

All this talk was about the beautiful, large two-story building on the corner of Bank street and 23rd, the place where I currently lived. I had been renting an apartment there for a year and eight months, but this block was already home to me long before I moved in. My parents were deeply rooted in this little section of Galveston.

Both of them were well-known in their own right, but they were famous for doing completely different things.

My father, "Easy" Billy Castro, was a world champion boxer who had a long, successful boxing career and finally retired when I was in high school. My mother was an artist who was best known for painting beach scenes in her own chunky style. She did a lot of light, bright island scenes, but my favorite paintings of hers were the darker ones—the night scenes.

I grew up around boxing and art. Some people might consider this an odd combination, but for me, it was a natural one. I turned out to be a dancer, so that was a third element to my personality. I was a ballerina who also loved martial arts and fine arts.

I hoped to bring them all together on our little section of Bank Street. There was a one-block stretch between 23rd and 24th Avenues, and I had spent most of my childhood going over there multiple times a week.

My father's boxing gym, a place called Bank Street Boxing, was situated on the south side of

Bank Street next to Carson's Diner, (where I was currently eating). My Aunt and Uncle owned a hardware store that was across the street from my dad's gym, and the building on the far side of King's Hardware was where I lived and where I hoped to open a new business.

"And your plan is to rent out Mister McCain's jewelry store and turn it into a dance studio?" she asked.

I nodded. "I want you to work with me, eventually, when you're done with school. I know you'll be working at the port and everything, and I know you'd need to think about it, but if you wanted to teach a class or two a week, I'd love for you to come work with me."

"Just let me get through college first," she said in an exasperated tone. "I have finals coming up soon, so right now, I can't imagine teaching a dance class."

"Oh, I know. You don't even live here right now. I was just saying, once you come back, and if you want to…"

"Thank you. It'd be cool to teach a class. Do you think you can afford eight-hundred on that rent?"

"Not at first," I said. "But eventually, yes. Definitely. I have a whole plan. There's going to be an art gallery in my dance studio. The studio *is* a gallery. I have it all worked out where I can sell artwork on commission and also run a studio. It's mixing both worlds that I love the most. I'll open it

12

sometimes after hours for showings. Of course, my mom will be the first artist featured."

"You always wanted to own a gallery," she said. "I remember you talking about that."

"It's because I can't do art myself," I said.

"You never tried hard enough," she said.

I smirked at her. "You sound like my mother. I know I didn't try very hard. I didn't love art, not doing it myself, at least. So, I don't regret not trying. I express myself through dance. I love other peoples' art, though. I know good art, and I feel like I could do well as a gallery owner."

"Well, you've convinced me," she said. "Now all that's left to do is convince your landlor... ord have mercy..." She trailed off.

Jesse had glanced outside several times since we'd been talking, but this time, something really caught her eye. I looked that way to find that it was a guy.

"Oh, my goodness. Goodness, gracious Tara. Look at that man... is he? Is he coming in here? Oh my gosh." She sat up straight, unabashedly staring out of the window, watching him. He was someone we didn't know—a tourist. This one was a little earlier than most, but the tourist season was just about to be in full swing and strangers would be everywhere. I did a double take, thinking he looked a little bit like Michael Connor, a guy we went to high school with. But no, it wasn't Michael. I glanced at Jesse, who was still busy staring. She turned and peered over her shoulder watching him the whole way down the sidewalk.

"He's coming in here," she whispered excitedly, glancing at me with wide eyes.

"I thought he was Michael Connor," I said with a dismissive shrug.

"Naw, what? He's waaaay finer than Michael Connor," Jesse said. "That guy would eat Michael Connor for breakfast."

"Let's hope not," I said.

"I'm just saying… he's about ten times finer than Michael. And probably like a hundred times smarter."

"Hey, I like Michael Connor," I said, taking up for our classmate. Jesse didn't mean any harm. We both knew she would date Michael Connor in a heartbeat. She was already boy crazy to begin with, but it had gotten worse since she went off to college. It was getting progressively worse year-by-year. She assumed she would find her future husband in Lubbock, preferably during her first three years of college. That hadn't happened yet, so now she seemed to notice every man who came around.

Chapter 2

Jesse kept looking at that guy the whole time we were eating. She was all excited about his friends, too, but it was really that first one who caught her eye. Just after he arrived, two other guys met him at his table. One of them looked like JoAnn Benson's older brother, Todd. Jesse and I thought it might be him, but we weren't sure. They talked to each other the whole time, and I really didn't care to speculate who they were. I would have never noticed them, honestly, but I couldn't help it with Jesse obsessing about them and giving me a play-by-play.

I was more preoccupied with my upcoming meeting. I couldn't wait to get my name on that lease downstairs. I pictured setting up my studio in that jewelry store. I could see it so clearly in my mind's eye. I already felt at home there.

That place was at least twice as big as it looked from the outside. Mr. McCain only kept the front part of it open. There was a big storage room in the back, which I would use for studio space, plus several closets and two office-sized rooms.

I had talked to Mister McCain about it quite a bit before he retired. He was happy that I would be the one taking it over, and he showed me all around and let me take measurements before he moved out. That storage room in the back was almost as big as the storefront, and I couldn't wait to get in there and see it now that those endless rows of shelves and boxes were out.

The whole place had beautiful wood floors that I was hoping to have refinished for a perfect dancing surface. I could see it all—dancers dressed out and lined up in an orderly row with artwork displayed on the walls. I was planning on painting it a soft, neutral color, either gray or tan.

"You're lost again," Jesse said, waving to get my attention. She had her purse on her shoulder and was already sitting on the edge of the seat like she was ready to stand up.

"I'm sorry," I said. "I was thinking about the wall color in the studio. Mom said there are some good whites out there, but I just keep picturing it gray."

"I say paint them gray, then. Do what you want." Jesse put her arm in mine as soon as I stood up from my place at the booth. "Come with me to the restroom," she said.

I was about to protest and say that I didn't need to use the restroom, but I realized that she probably didn't need to use it either, and she was just looking for an excuse to walk by that table of guys.

We said goodbye to Maggie as we walked toward the restroom for an unnecessary pitstop. It was crowded in the diner, and Jesse got away with staring at their table without having them notice at all.

"Did you see him? Oh, my flipping goodness!" She whispered to me as we rounded the corner.

"Two of them were cute but that one guy, gosh, Tara. Did you see him? I've definitely never seen him before. He must be friends with JoAnn Benson's brother, though, because I'm pretty sure that's who was wearing the blue shirt. Todd. Todd Benson."

"You are a mess," I said. I stopped in my tracks and lifted the box of leftovers that I was holding. "I'm not going in there with this," I said, gesturing to the restroom door. "I need to go. I wanted to run upstairs and put this in the fridge before my meeting."

"Okay, I seriously need to go to the restroom. But good luck with your landlord. Where are you meeting him? In the jewelry store?"

I smiled. "Yeah, soon to be dance studio. I'm taking a camera with me. I'll snap some pictures while I'm in there with him."

She made a little squealing noise and excitement as she reached out to hug me. "I'll see you in a couple of months," she said since she was headed back to Lubbock later today.

"Okay, do good on your finals."

"I will," she said. "Do good on your meeting."

"Thank you."

I walked down the hallway and out of the restaurant. I didn't so much as spare a glance at Todd Benson's table on my way out. I waved at two people I knew at other tables, but I was focused and didn't stop to chat with anyone.

I left the diner through the door on the corner and walked up the south side of the street, passing the windows of the diner before going past my father's boxing gym. I peered inside and could see my father in the back, working with a few guys. I didn't go in or try to get his attention. I kept walking, past the small seamstress shop before crossing the street. Technically, I was jay walking, but no one was around, and this stretch of Bank Street felt like my living room, anyway.

I waved at Mister Randall who was standing on the sidewalk near my aunt and uncle's hardware store. Just past the hardware store was where my building started. First was the doorway that led to the Seabreeze Apartments. There was a door with an awning which opened into an entryway with three mailboxes and a set of stairs going up to apartments 201, 202, and 203. (Mine was 201.)

Right next to the door that led to the Seabreeze was where the old jewelry store began. There were windows lining two sides of the building, but the door to the store was situated on Bank Street, not far from the door to my apartment. I would literally have to walk ten feet to work. I could hardly believe this store was now gloriously vacant and about to be mine. I glanced inside before I went upstairs, imagining it with bars and mirrors instead of that big u-shaped counter that took up the entire floor right now.

My dad had already looked at it and said he could help me take it out before we got the floors refinished. Mister McCain wasn't able to promise the place to me, but he was sure I'd get it. He left a note for the landlord, putting in a good word for me and my family, so we were sure he would rent it to me.

I was at home on this corner, and I was elated with how things were working out. I was nervous about paying the rent in addition to the rent on my apartment, but I had already talked to my parents, and they were willing to help me until the business gained momentum. Plus, I figured maybe I could ask the landlord for a discount, seeing as how I was renting two places from him.

I only took a few seconds to glance inside before I went into the door that lead to my apartment. I walked up the stairs and circled back to apartment 201. It was the best of the three. They were all nice, but mine overlooked Bank Street and the corner. It would be a dream come true to live here and own the business downstairs. I was just getting started with all of this, and it already felt like I had everything I could ever want.

I didn't want to be too early, so I stayed in my apartment for ten minutes before walking downstairs for the big meeting. I took some things with me—a camera, some photos of my old dance studio, and some photos of ideas I had for a new one. I even made him a little booklet to take back to Tennessee so he knew exactly what was going on in his building. I was as prepared as I'd ever be.

I checked my reflection several times before I walked downstairs. There was a clock downstairs near the mailboxes, and it told me that I was three minutes early, which seemed perfect. I hadn't seen William Harper in the store when I walked by a few minutes before, but I hoped he'd be there by now.

He wasn't. I tried to open the front door of the store when I got downstairs, and sure enough, it was locked.

My father's name was William, and so was my brother's. They went by Billy and Will, but it was still a cool coincidence that they shared a name with my landlord, and I thought it would be one of the first conversation points I would hit once I met Mister Harper.

I peered into the storefront, smiling and planning how it would all go down.

"It's closed," I heard a man say from behind me. I turned. It was the man from the restaurant—the one Jesse had been checking out.

"Oh, I know it's closed," I said. "Are you talking about the jewelry store? I know it's closed. I actually have a meeting in here. I'm waiting for the guy who owns this building."

"I'm the guy who owns this building," he said, with an easy smile. He was young, and he had on jeans and a t-shirt with sandals, and I smiled, knowing he was kidding around. It crossed my mind that he was hitting on me. I was all dressed up after all.

"What's your name, then?" I asked.

"Trey Harper."

"I'm here to meet William Harper. Are you his son or something?"

"Yes. But technically, I'm William, too," he said. "It's just nobody ever calls me that."

He casually walked up to the door and unlocked it. I watched him, my heart pounding. It wasn't that he was young and handsome. I couldn't care less about that. It was that he was the owner of this building. My ever-loving fate was in his hands.

"I thought I was meeting Mrs. Harper's son."

"I am Mrs. Harper's son," he said, cutting his eyes at me playfully. "But the Mrs. Harper you're thinking of… Joan Harper… the lady who used to live here… I'm her great-grandson. Her son was the first William. I'm the third. Hence the name Trey."

"Huh." I made a sound in my chest, indicating that I was listening to him and that I thought his story was interesting. But I was too busy processing everything. Was he the actual owner of this building? I still wasn't understanding. I walked into the empty store, and he followed me, turning on lights even though there was a lot of light coming in through the windows.

"Is your dad coming?" I asked.

"My dad's playing golf in Brentwood, Tennessee right now. Why?"

"Oh, I thought he was my landlord. William. Is he the owner, or are you?"

Trey was moving around, turning on lights and looking at things. "I am," he said. "And I am so relieved that I came down here. My family was all wrong about this place."

He groaned a little as he opened some drapes that were covered in dust and looked like they hadn't been open in years. Dust flew everywhere, and he backed up, instinctually covering his nose with his t-shirt. I did the same, stepping back and covering my nose even though I was halfway across the room. He let out a little humorless laugh as he looked at me, somewhat astonished.

"I thought this place was a dump all along. My great-grandmother passed away two years ago. I got a letter from a lawyer saying she left me this property. It's a long story, but for several reasons, I assumed this was a dump of a building in Podunk, Texas, and I wanted nothing to do with it other than to cash the rent checks. Joan had a falling out with my grandpa, and none of us knew her growing up." He paused and gestured around himself smiling. "I thought she was a crazy old lady. I thought this was going to be something on the verge of being condemned, until I got here and realized this place isn't bad at all. It's a great little town, and the building's amazing. Way better than I expected. I wasn't even getting two thousand a month for rent on this whole building, so I just assumed it was in shambles." He let out a little humorless laugh. "I'm so glad I came." He stopped walking and took a deep breath standing in the middle of the room and looking around and filling his lungs with the scent of possibility. "Now I'm thinking maybe my great-grandmother wasn't so bad after all. Maybe she just knew nothing about managing real estate."

"Oh, so, are you going to make changes?" I asked, trying not to seem mortified.

"Oh, yeah, absolutely. I knew the rent had to go up when I first got here, but I wasn't sure how much. I didn't know much about the market in Galveston. But I was just talking to a real estate agent who said I could get at least double what I was getting for these places."

"Double for what places?"

"This storefront and the apartments upstairs. There's three of them up there."

"I know."

"Oh, you do?"

"Yes. I live there."

"You do?"

"Yes, I, I thought you knew that. I'm a tenant upstairs, but I'm also here to talk to you about renting this space down here."

"Oh, well the price just went waaaay up," he said.

He was being happy and lighthearted, and I felt more like I was lightheaded.

"I, I'm Tara Castro," I said, trying to switch gears, sound confident, distract him, convince him that he didn't need more money. "I live upstairs. I rent apartment 201 right there." I pointed upward since I was currently standing under my bedroom. "I'm a long-standing member of this community. I love this city, and especially this block we're on right here. My dad is a boxer. His gym is—"

"I know. It's across the street. I already went by there. Easy Billy Castro. I didn't even realize he was from Texas."

"You know of him?" I asked.

"Yes."

"Well, I'm his daughter, Tara."

"I knew that, too."

"How?"

"I had lunch with a real estate agent just now. You were over there. I asked about you, and he told me who you were."

"Is Todd Benson selling real estate now?"

"No, Todd's a contractor. It was the other guy, Justin."

When he said that name, I figured out that it was a guy named Justin Harrison, but I didn't say anything. I was stunned. I wasn't expecting to walk into an honest monologue where he announced that he was going to be raising the rent. And now, I had told him who I was, and it didn't seem like that was going to change things. I went from feeling excited and hopeful to frustrated and hopeless. It was truly amazing how feelings change so quickly.

"Were you talking about raising the rent on my apartment?" I asked, blinking at him.

The dust had mostly settled, but I got caught staring at a few particles that were floating in the air between us.

"Oh, no, not right this minute. I'm going to honor your contract amount until the lease is up."

"I've only got, like, four months left."

"Yeah, one of them, the guy in 202, has a month left, then you have four months. The couple in the back, they just signed theirs. They have ten months."

"Stan, in apartment 202, only has a month?"

"Yeah, but that one couple just renewed." He breathed a defeated sigh. "I wish I would have come here before that happened. I thought I was *thankful* to have them renew, so I didn't change anything, but they've been raking me over the coals this whole time!"

"Nobody's raking you over coals. Stan's been living in that apartment for ten years."

"Exactly, and only paying three hundred dollars a month. What the heck? It's no wonder he doesn't leave. I mean, of course, I'll give him first dibs on staying in the place if he wants to sign again, but the rent is going up. There's no question about it. This whole building—I can get double the rent in the condition it's in. Justin was saying that if I do a few renovations, I can get even more than that."

"What about down here? The jewelry store?"

"He said fourteen to sixteen hundred in the shape it's in. More if we fix it up. That's why I was talking to Todd."

My heart was pounding and I had no idea what to say. I felt like I was in a dream. I expected this meeting to go so completely different. I was reeling. I didn't expect him to be young and in sandals. I didn't expect him to say any of this.

"I don't think the rent here goes as high as it does in Nashville, though. We were used to paying this amount."

He laughed. "I'm sure you were," he said.

"What, so, you're just going to kick us out if we don't agree to pay the higher amount?"

He gave me a sideways look, smiling a little like he must be missing something. "That's usually how it works," he said slowly.

Chapter 3

I felt utterly heartbroken, and this was only the first three minutes of my meeting with Mister Harper—if you could even call it a meeting. Basically, he was nonchalantly informing me that I was being kicked out of my apartment.

I was so frustrated that I could barely even think about not getting to rent the business. I couldn't have this. I already had it all planned out. I didn't have a plan B.

"Mister McCain was willing to sign his lease again and just let me move in and take over the rent," I said, regretting the fact that I ever called him in the first place. "And Ms. Gwendolyn's Dance Academy is a long-standing tradition here. My studio would be under her umbrella. I'm calling it something different, but I have Miss Gwendolyn's blessing, and she's even going to be sending some students my way—the ones who are driving from Jamaica Beach, you know. So, it's a really great business plan. I have it all mapped out. I was planning on making this place into a dance academy and part-time art gallery."

He stared blankly at me, looking like he was trying to process everything I was saying. I had no idea what he was going to say.

"I'd be happy to have you rent this place and turn it into a dance academy, if that's what you're proposing. I'd honestly rather give it to you than to Burger Time or 7 Eleven. If you can pay the rent, it's yours."

"Burger Time or 7 Eleven? Where did they come from?"

"My grandparents and parents are all into real estate. They have a ton of property in Tennessee. I bought a carwash when I turned seventeen, and I've been into it ever since. Anyway, I can tell that sort of business would want to rent this corner easily. My uncle owns eight franchises of Burger Time. I mentioned that to Todd, and he said one of those would go over well here."

I put my hand up to get him to stop talking. I felt speechless, breathless. "Just wait a second," I said calmly, rationally. "Why would Todd Benson tell you it's acceptable to have a burger restaurant right here? Did he say that?"

"Yeah, why? He said it'd go over great with all this foot traffic from the strand."

"It *would* go over great," I said, staring at him. "That's why it's already been done. By Mister Carson… who opened the diner where you were just eating. They *are* a burger place."

Trey smiled and shrugged, shaking his head. "Great, then I hope you rent it from me. You seem to already have a vision, and I'm fine with not renting it to a franchise. You can open whatever you want down here as long as you pay the rent on the first of the month."

"Which is how much?"

"Well, don't quote me on this, because there are still some variables. I need to see how much needs to be done, and what's going on upstairs, but down here, this will be in the ballpark of fifteen to eighteen."

"Fifteen to eighteen what?" I asked.

"Hundred."

"*Dollars a month?*" I asked.

"Yes." He nodded, looking at me with no shame or regret whatsoever, like that was completely reasonable.

I let out a huffing, scoff sound that was completely involuntary. "We're talking about people's lives here," I said.

"Mostly it's just your life and my life," he said with a little smile.

"And everyone upstairs—Stan, and Mickey and Charlotte in the back."

He stared at me for several seconds, wearing a serious expression. He shrugged a little, looking like he was attempting to be regretful.

"I told you, I'm going to honor your leases," he said.

"Yeah, but then, after that, you're just raising the rent by double?"

"Yes," he said, not seeing a problem.

"Is that legal?"

He let out a little laugh. "Yes. It's perfectly legal. It's my building. I can charge whatever I want for rent. It's your choice whether or not you want to pay it. In fact, if you want to talk about legal and illegal, that whole plan about you taking over the jeweler's lease... that's called subletting, and it's illegal. It's goes against his contract. He can't do that."

"Well, he's obviously not going to," I said, defensively.

I was angry and, honestly, embarrassed. I stared at him. "How can you just come in here and be so nonchalant with this?" I asked.

He stared straight at me. He had a laidback vibe up until now, but as he stared at me, his dark brown eyes were a little more penetrating, serious. "How can you stand here and seriously think that I would take half of what something's worth? As far as I'm concerned, you should have told me that I was charging you far too little for rent. As far as I'm concerned, you've been taking advantage of me this whole time."

I scoffed. "It's not my fault that you don't care enough to come over here. I don't own any buildings in other towns. If I did, I'd probably *check on them every once in a while.*"

"Well, you should be thankful I didn't because rent would have doubled long ago."

He was speaking to me reasonably, but I blinked at him, holding back tears and feeling shaken.

"I know this isn't the best time. But I do need to go upstairs and check out your apartment sometime while I'm here. It doesn't have to be today, but maybe tomorrow."

I just stared. I blinked. I wanted desperately to say something spiteful, but I couldn't make myself do it. I wasn't even sure what I would say.

"I-I'm not done down here," I said. "I thought we were meeting. But, I mean, yeah, it's your building, so you can go up whenever you want, obviously, but I thought we were still meeting to let me look at this space down here. I was going to take pictures."

"Is this still a possibility for you?" he asked, looking hopeful, happy. "I figure your dad could co-sign."

He knew my father had a successful career, and that was the truth, but I would never ask him to pay that amount—especially with my apartment rent going up. My mind was so busy doing math and thinking of all the possibilities, that I got lost in thought, staring blankly at this guy who had come in and wrecked my world.

"My dad's not going to… I really thought that this whole thing was God, and… uhhhh, so, let's just… uhh… first of all, we need to figure out what you're asking for both places."

"That's what this trip is all about," he said. He walked behind the jewelry counter. "I'll be here for a few more days, taking notes and making plans. I'll have a better idea about rent after I get some bids and give it a little thought."

"So, I'm supposed to just wait on pins and needles, not knowing what the price is going to be?"

"I can tell you it's going to be a lot more than it is now."

"Can't you just... (I was grasping at straws.) ... raise it slower? A hundred dollars a year, and then just year-by-year go up instead of all at once—"

"A hundred dollars a year?" he said like that was the craziest thing he'd ever heard.

"Not a hundred for the whole year, but a hundred a month more for the duration of the year. With the upstairs, maybe you could go up to four hundred for year, and then next year you could raise it to five? Slowly like that. Why can't you do that?"

"I guess the answer is that I could, theoretically, do that. I just wish you could see where that really doesn't make sense on my end. If Stan can't make the six hundred for rent, someone else will. You asking me to take four hundred is basically asking me to give someone two hundred dollars a month."

I was so mad and embarrassed that I had no response for him. "Mrs. Harper obviously didn't want it this way."

"I guess you're right," he said with a shrug. "But she's not making these decisions anymore. I'm sorry, but I'm not going to charge one group of people half the rent just because they were paying that before. The rent goes up in places. That's just how life is." He paused and smiled at me. "I have a property in

Nashville where I've raised the rent five times since I've owned it."

"Well, that's not very nice of you."

"Well it's not very nice of you to say that I should get less of something just because you're the one who's giving it to me. You're not telling all these other people on this block that they're charging too much for rent. You only care because it pertains to you."

"I know everybody on this block, and they don't pay too much for rent," I said.

It was a lie. I wasn't lying that I knew everyone on the block, but I had no idea how much they paid for their places. I was relatively sure people I knew owned their buildings and didn't rent.

"Why don't you just sell it?" I asked. The question came out of my mouth as soon as the thought crossed my mind, and I'll honestly say it was a glorious moment for me.

Of course!

I would buy it.

My parents would buy it.

The more I thought about it, the more excited I became. "Just sell it to me. You don't want it, anyway."

"I never said that," he said. He kept moving around, looking places, adjusting things.

I walked with him, coming to stand a few feet from him as he moved. "You live out of state," I reminded him. "You don't want a building all the

33

way over here in Texas. And, like you said… in your mind, this place was in shambles, anyway. You might as well just sell it to someone who wants it and loves it and would take care of it and live here for the rest of her life."

He stuttered, opening his mouth closing it again, hesitating, not wanting to say the wrong thing. He put his hands up in a gesture of surrender. "I'm sorry, Miss, uh, Castro. I wasn't expecting to have this conversation with you. I have a lady who returns my business calls for me, and I don't think I realized that the person I was meeting this afternoon was also a tenant upstairs."

"I told her I was," I said.

"She mentioned that I'd be meeting a tenant, but I didn't realize that was today. I have a few other meetings."

"Are you meeting with other people?" I asked.

"Uh-huh," he said, still looking around, checking the place out.

"Are you meeting other people who want to rent this place?" I asked, feeling desperate.

"Not yet. Right now, I'm just talking to inspectors and appraisers. My father lectured me about not having all of that done two years ago. He wasn't even sure how it's possible that it was signed over to me without all of that happening. Maybe it was God helping you have low rent for this long. Maybe you should look at it that way."

Trey kept walking around, looking. I knew I should relent. I knew I should just tell him to think about the new amount and let me know what it was. But I couldn't hold my tongue.

"I'd really like you to consider selling it," I said. I looked at him with a serious, pleading expression, and he tilted his head at me, smiling like he was slightly confused.

"Why don't you get one of these other people to sell their building?" he said. "Why mine? I already told you, I like it here. I think it's a cool little city. I never said I wanted to sell this building."

I held my shoulders back and my chin up and let out a little resigned sigh. "Well, keep me in mind, please. At least think about it. Think about selling."

He gave me a regretful smile. "I'll tell you right now. I don't want you to be mad at me, but I also don't want you to get your hopes up. I don't plan on selling it." He glanced around looking up at the ornamental tile on the ceiling. "I like this place. Thanks for the offer, but I don't think it's for sale."

I wanted to do something crazy like stomp my feet and throw a fit and say, "I want it more than yoooou!" But I just took a deep breath, keeping my composure, staring blankly at him.

Chapter 4

Trey Harper

"Would you like to look around still?" Trey asked the question after a long awkward pause. He had just informed Tara that the building wasn't for sale. "I'd love to have you rent it," he added. "It'd be great as a dance and art studio, like you were saying. It's probably a lot less smelly than a burger joint, so I'd love to have you move in."

"I would love to rent it," she said. "I just hope I can afford it." She took a breath, but then continued speaking. "And, yes, I'd love to take a look around." She turned and stared straight at him like she had an idea. "We can trade places, if you want."

"What's that mean?" he asked.

"You could go look around upstairs while I stay down here. I don't really care about being upstairs while you're in there, so if you want to look around, you might as well go now. I have a tape measure in my bag, so I'll just take a few measurements in case things end up working out."

He made an expression like her offer took him by surprise. "I don't mind you looking around down here and measuring, but I don't need to go upstairs right this minute. I wasn't going to spring that on you. I'm going to call you and the other tenants later this afternoon and try to set something up for tomorrow."

"It's all the same to me," she said.

She had been wearing a smile when they first met, but she lost it. Trey knew she didn't like him very much. He might not like himself if he was in her situation, but to him, things were cut and dry.

This was his inheritance.

Sure, he had underestimated it at first, but that didn't mean he had to continue to lose money. It would be unwise of him to let the tenants stay there at this price when a higher price was clearly fair.

"It's fine if you want to go upstairs," she said. "Now's as good a time as any. I'm busy tomorrow, anyway." She opened her notebook and spread it along with a few other things onto the counter.

"I don't want to intrude."

"I really don't mind," she said. But she was lying. She did mind. She was just being friendly. Barely. If he was going to go in her apartment at all, she would rather get it over with.

Trey watched as she reached out and handed him her keys. There were five or six of them on the ring, and she didn't specify which one would open her door. She was obviously leaving it to him to figure that out.

"It's number 201," she said in a matter-of-fact tone.

"Are you sure?" he asked. "Because I don't have to go now. I'm not in a hurry."

"The faster you go up there, the faster you'll know what my rent is going to be, right?"

"Y-yes."

"So, I'm good with you going up there now. That way I can get my head straight about where I'm going to live and what I'm going to do."

She was stone cold. All the hope and brightness and joy had left her face. It was like she finally realized that Trey was keeping the building and that he was serious about raising the rent. He thought about it as he walked out of the jewelry store and onto the sidewalk. He felt bad for the woman, but then he reminded himself that she was being completely unreasonable. First, she had been paying way too little for rent this whole time, and now, she was going to be mad when he told her he was going to do the fair thing and raise it. He huffed and puffed about it under his breath as he climbed the stairs.

Three hundred dollars was nothing for this place. His great-grandmother probably hadn't raised the rent in decades. He hated to raise it so drastically, but good grief, what did these people expect? This had gone on far too long. He looked around when he got to the top of the stairs. The stairs, the rail, and the lower part of the walls were wood that had been stained dark mahogany. It could use some cleaning and basic maintenance, but the bones were great.

He glanced at the doors for the other two apartments before he made it to Tara's. He had a key to each of the apartments on his own keyring—the one Joan Harper had left for him. But Trey went for Tara's keys instead. There were twelve different keys on his building set, and all of the keys were the same brand, but Tara's keys were all different so it was easy to find a match on hers based on the brand of his. Trey found the correct key on the first try.

He opened the door, smiling at the sight of her apartment. Oh, gosh. Three hundred? No way. He hadn't expected this. It was eclectic and colorful with paintings and furniture that was all different colors. She had a picture in her notebook. He saw her idea for a ballet studio downstairs, and it was nothing like this apartment.

This place was huge also. He looked around, marveling at how big it was. He knew it was the largest apartment of the three, but the ceilings were high, and it was more spacious than he imagined. Tara had it decorated beautifully.

He stood in the living room, looking around for a long minute, and having a new appreciation for just how much this building was worth. He chastised himself inwardly for being so distracted and judgmental that he let this place slip through his fingers for two years. He assumed this building wasn't worthy of his time and attention, and he was so wrong. It was a humbling experience to stand there in an apartment that he himself would be happy to live in. He felt ashamed of himself for missing out on all the money that could have been made since he inherited the property. Trey was intelligent, and there was no excuse for something this big slipping past him.

He felt humbled as he gazed around at her apartment. The ceilings had to be twelve feet high. She had gorgeous paintings on the wall. They were evening and sunset scenes in bright colors and jewel tones. They were professionally framed and looked like they belonged in the home of a collector.

Trey walked over to the large window that was positioned on the far side of the living room. He meant to glance out of it, but he got caught staring and stayed there for several minutes. He found that it was quite relaxing, staring out at Bank Street from this perspective. He could see action in several places—as far down as the diner on one corner, and the other way, toward the office building on the adjacent block.

Tara had personal pictures set up in frames on a shelf that was near the window. Trey wasn't meaning to snoop. In fact, he was trying *not* to snoop. But he couldn't help but take a glance at the photographs. They were a beautiful family, and they took interesting photographs. There were photos of them with art, dancing, and fighting. There were no standard family photographs where they posed in a studio. Trey thought that was interesting since that was the only thing on the shelf at his house. He had his own place in Nashville, and he only had one picture of his family on display. It was one his mother had given them, and it was a very posed picture.

He loved his family. He had two siblings, a brother and a sister. Both of his siblings were married, and their spouses and children were also in the picture. It was nothing like this.

There was a black and white photograph of Tara as a little girl, hugging her father who was bleeding and swollen, battle scarred after a fight. Trey didn't mean to continue looking at them. He kept telling himself to look away. But they were all so interesting. There were at least ten framed photographs, and the people in them were so full of life and originality. Trey wondered what sort of town this was and what sort of family he had found there.

He glanced out of the window again, looking in the direction of the boxing gym. There was a small hand painted sign mounted above the door, hanging from the top where it could swing in the wind.

Bank Street

Boxing

He watched someone walk in the door. It was a guy with a duffle bag slung over his shoulder, and Trey imagined that he was a boxer going to train. This whole place was just... interesting. Tara was interesting. She was a black-haired beauty. Black Beauty, just like the horse. Tara reminded Trey of a wild horse, like a mustang, tough and a little unpredictable.

He gazed out the window and at her candid photographs, thinking this whole experience was the most unexpected thing he could have encountered in this building. He looked around, feeling happy and at home, and then somehow his thoughts turned around and he wound up thinking that if a person could afford to have such a nice apartment with such nice things, then she could certainly afford to pay more for rent.

There were several antique pieces of furniture that went well with her other décor. The living room was huge, and it felt warm with all of her bright eclectic things meticulously placed around. He looked in the bathroom. It smelled like fruit— peaches, maybe. Or raspberries. Her place was clean with just the right amount of organized clutter that made it feel lived-in and warm. The bathroom was painted light purple with the wainscoting done in white. His eye fell onto her bottle of perfume, and he almost squinted to read the name, but he didn't let himself do it. He was here to see the apartment.

Trey snapped his attention to the shower where he noticed the curtain and faucet. His eyes roamed over the cabinetry and counter tops, taking in other things that had nothing to do with perfume. It was a two-bedroom place, and he went into bedroom number one. It was obviously the master because Tara's personal things were in there. Again, there were things lying around, and it was obvious that the place was lived in, but it was clean and inviting.

There were other personal pictures in the bedroom, and Trey glanced at them, but he did it so quickly that he hardly got to take them in. He didn't think Tara had a husband or boyfriend. The guy that was in most of her pictures seemed to be her brother. It didn't matter. He barely took in the details of her bedroom before he walked out. It was nice in there, and it had two windows that looked over different streets since it was on the corner. The bed was huge and way too inviting, and Trey got out of there quickly and peeked into the second bedroom.

There wasn't a bed in that one. There was a small desk against one wall with a boombox on the floor. But besides that, the entire floor was open. He knew Tara danced in that room because there was a huge mirror mounted to the wall and also one of those bars that you hold onto.

This was not a three-hundred-dollar apartment. It bugged him that this place existed and he had no idea. It was his own fault. He should have never assumed things about his great-grandmother or been so passive about his inheritance.

He had mistakenly relied on the maintenance guy. He was the only person who had been the go-between. Trey paid him every month to look after the building and tend to any of the tenant's needs. He had been Trey's only contact in Galveston. Trey thought about that maintenance guy and how he, himself, deserved more than Trey was paying him for basic duties on a building this size. Everything needed to go up, the rent and the paycheck for the maintenance guy. The expectations set for his building were too low. It was an old gem on a cool corner of the city.

Trey went back into Tara's living room, hoping and praying that all of the apartments were this well-kept. He breathed in the smell, taking one last look around and feeling satisfied. He loved it there, and he regretted that it took him this long to find that out.

Chapter 5

Tara Castro
A month later

Trey Harper was not messing around. He began planning and investing in the building right away. I saw him a few more times during his first trip to Galveston, but he never gave me a definitive answer about the rent for downstairs. He called me before he left town and said that he hadn't decided what to price it at yet. He said he might want to do some work on it while it was vacant. He promised that he would let me be the first to know once he was ready to lease it to someone.

So, my business venture plans were on hold, at least for now.

I went back to my life as it was, working at Dad's gym and Miss Gwendolyn's dance studio. Between my duties at the gym and actually working out there, I was at Bank Street Boxing about thirty hours a week. Even in my big plan, when I imagined running my own dance studio and art gallery, I knew I would still work with my dad. I loved working there.

I decided the logical thing to do with my building and apartment situation was to see what else was out there. I inquired about several other properties, and to my own dismay, I found out that Trey had been correct. The only places I could find to rent for eight-hundred-dollars were either tiny, run down, or on the outskirts of town. There were no nice storefronts in the downtown area going for less than fourteen hundred, and certainly none as nice as the jewelry store. The same was true for my apartment. In the last month, I had looked at several other places, and none were as nice as the one where I lived for the price. I felt a little bad for being so cold to Trey when he gave me the news.

It didn't seem to faze him, though. He just moved along with his plans without giving much thought to my situation. A week after he visited Galveston, he started improvements on the outside of the building. It was being washed and painted. He had chosen a similar color, a stone greyish-green color that was similar to but richer than the one that had been on there before. It seemed more stately now, with the exterior walls and trim getting repainted.

Next to Stan's apartment, there was a closet with a staircase to the roof access. I vaguely knew it was there, but I never had access to it before. Trey had cleaned up the rooftop when he was in town to see the progress. I ran into him when he was going in there one day, and he said I could use the rooftop as long as I kept the door locked.

Later that day, I found a key in an envelope that had been slipped under my door. I didn't see Trey again on that trip, but I was thankful I had run into him. I liked having access to the rooftop, and I wouldn't have a key if I hadn't run into him in the hall. I knew that because neither of my neighbors got a key. I didn't tell them about mine.

So, for a while, my life didn't change. If anything, it got better. I was excited that Trey seemed to love the building, and I got lost in the comfort of being able to stay there and enjoy the improvements while paying the same, low rent.

But suddenly, I was reminded of the grim reality of being kicked out when Stan, my neighbor in 202, started moving his things out. I was on my way to Carson's to pick up breakfast when I noticed him in the hallway, instructing a couple of guys who were carrying a table. We had a whole conversation where he informed me that his rent had gone up to six-fifty, and that he would have to either get a roommate or move out. He said he was so used to living by himself that a roommate wasn't an option.

Stan was tired, and he was in the middle of moving to a place that was half as nice. Needless to say, he wasn't very happy. We talked about Trey a little bit and how it would've been nice if he would have raised the rent slowly, but ultimately, both of us knew it was his building and that we didn't have a say in the matter. I felt for Stan, though. It was extremely easy to put myself into his shoes because I would literally be there soon.

That first month of normalcy was just great, but having Stan move out put a cloud of dread over me.

It was a week later when I ran into Trey Harper again. I was on my way to the gym, and I noticed that the door to the old jewelry store was open. Of course, I peered inside, and when I saw that it was Trey, I walked a little closer.

Trey wasn't the only one inside. I could see, as I came to the door, that some construction was going on. There were two men dressed in work clothes. They were pointing at the ceiling and talking to each other.

I hated confrontation and I had a bad habit of rushing to the point, which was exactly what I did in that moment. I was nervous, and without greeting Trey in any other way, I just said, "What's going on? Is someone moving in down here?"

"Hello to you, too, Tara," he said. "And no. I told you I'd let you know when I'm ready to lease it. These guys are going to take these counters out. They're not original, they're from the sixties. I think it would be better to have it open in here."

I just nodded. I wanted to say that it was a mistake to do too much work on it since I was willing to do all of that for free. But, honestly, I didn't think I could afford to move in here, even without renovations. I knew my chances were slim.

"Stan moved out," I said, unable to stop myself from saying everything off the bat.

"Yes, he did," Trey agreed. He had been looking at notes in a folder, but he looked up from what he was doing to have this conversation with me. Twice he had glanced down at my legs. He tried not to, but his eyes got drawn to the fact that I had on shorts. I was on my way to the gym to work out. I knew my shorts were short, and I put my duffle bag strategically in front of me when I caught Trey glance at me.

"Who's moving in there?" I asked, wondering how quickly he could find someone to pay the new, higher amount.

"I'm not looking for somebody right away. I'm having a few things fixed. I'll stay up there while I'm here for a few days and kind of take stock of what needs to happen and how soon I want to get it rented out."

I shook my head at his nonchalance. I was scared for myself and thinking of my own future fate when I said, "It's just weird that you're not even worried about getting someone else in there right away, and yet you wouldn't just let Stan stay there. It seems better to let him stay there for the amount that he was paying than to make him move out and not get any money for that place at all."

Trey grinned at me, shaking his head as he casually came my way. "It is hilarious that you try to tell me what I should and shouldn't do with my building. Nobody is telling you what you should do with your stuff. You have an empty bedroom in your apartment right now. I saw it for myself. It's got mirrors in it. Why don't you put a bed in there and let Stan stay with you if you are so worried about Stan having to move out?"

I blinked at him. I was stunned. He was right, and I had nothing to say in response, so I just turned and walked away. My eyes were wide and I wasn't smiling as I just slowly turned on my heels and began walking out of the store.

I heard his footsteps as he crossed the room behind me. "Tara," he said.

By the time I stopped and turned around, he was only a few feet from me. He was dressed in jeans and a t-shirt with skater shoes. He didn't look like the owner of a building. I would have imagined him on a skateboard at the boardwalk and not cashing rent checks and making construction upgrades.

"I didn't mean to offend you," he said when I turned.

"You didn't. You're actually really right. It's your building. I shouldn't have..." I trailed off, not knowing how to put into words what I wanted to say. "I shouldn't have bugged you about it. I'm sorry." I spoke humbly, knowing I was wrong in this situation.

I wanted to tell him that I was only saying these things because I was terrified of being in Stan's situation and knew I would find myself there in just a few months. I wanted to spew my guts and say all that, but I held my tongue. I had already done enough to let him know he was inconveniencing all of us. I gave him a little bow and turned again.

"Are you going out in those shorts?" he asked.

I turned, looking at him with an instant offended glare that said you must not be talking to me.

He gave me a serious nod and gestured to my body. "Your shorts are really short," he said.

I let out a scoff, smiling since he must have been joking.

"You probably shouldn't go over to that boxing gym wearing those."

I tilted my head at him. "Are you trying to teach me a lesson about what it feels like for people to tell you what to do with your stuff? Because I just said I was sorry for that."

He gave me a confused glare like he was trying to understand what I was saying. "No. I'm just saying your shorts are really short, and there's a bunch of guys over there. You shouldn't wear them in there unless you want that kind of attention."

I didn't know what to say. I thought he was doing this on purpose, to say I was being annoying about his building. But he was seriously worried about my shorts.

"It's hot in the gym," I said. "This is what I wear all the time."

Trey stared downward with a small apologetic smile. "I'm not... I also wanted to say, that I'm not kicking you out right away." He shifted his stance and then glanced at me. "I'll work with you on the rent increase for your apartment. I know you like being here with your dad's place right across the street and everything, and I don't want you to think that I'm going to be inflexible in three months when it's time to sign again."

I was already moving to walk out of the door. I was on my way to a boxing class that happened at 10am. I was expected to be there to partner up with a young featherweight fighter named Miguel who was improving quickly. I had been working with him a lot lately. My younger brother, Will, would have normally done it, but he was out with a fractured hand.

I smiled broadly at Trey. "I have to get to work but I'm pretty sure I want more information about the things you just said. I don't know what you were saying, exactly, but I think it feels like a little bit of good news, so I'd like to talk to you more about that." I spoke ineloquently as I backed toward the door, and Trey smiled at me. "Seriously," I said. "If what you were saying is real, then, thank you."

"You're welcome," he said.

But he was calling it at my back because we had already waved at each other and I was in the process of leaving.

I walked across the street feeling happy and oh so relieved. I was smiling at the thought of being able to stay in the apartment after my lease was up.

I luxuriated for a moment, but then I got mad at myself for being so charmed. I thought back to Trey telling me I should have Stan stay in my extra bedroom, and I felt embarrassed by the memory of that exchange. One second, I was feeling thankful to Trey, and the next, I felt like I hated him. I thought about him talking about my shorts, too, and my cheeks felt hot at the memory of it. My father always got on to me when I had on short shorts. I wasn't trying to get attention from guys when I did it. I think Dad knew that, and he let me get away with it even though they weren't his favorite. I was just comfortable in them and thought they looked good on me. I was raised as a dancer, so I moved well in light, fitted clothes

I wasn't even expecting to run into Trey, anyway. And it wasn't like I owed him an explanation about my clothing. I had thoughts like these as I walked toward the gym.

But once I got there, it was business as usual. For the next two hours, I worked out and trained with Miguel.

Chapter 6

The door for apartment 202 was wide open when I finished working at the gym that day. I knew that because I had to pass by there on the way to my apartment. I heard men's voices as I passed, and I walked by the open door without even looking inside. I had my hands full so it took me a second to search for my key and open my door. I heard them saying something about knocking down a wall, and I cringed knowing that every construction project meant more money.

I took a shower the instant I walked into my apartment. I was dripping with sweat. My protective father was not at the gym this morning, so I had trained a little harder with Miguel.

There was a piece of paper that had been slipped under my door when I got out of the shower. I almost didn't notice it, but once I did, I went right over to it, picked it up, and read it. It was a handwritten note.

I will be in apartment 202 all afternoon.
Please come by when you get the chance.

Trey signed it with his first name.

I turned it over, noticing that it was a receipt from my aunt and uncle's hardware store.

I went over to the apartment immediately. I was so anxious to hear whatever he had to say that I just started walking over there that instant. I didn't even think about the fact that I had on lounge clothes with my hair wrapped in a towel. I realized I should have considered my condition when I was about halfway there, and I reached up and took my hair out of the towel while I was in the hallway. I held the towel in my hand as I leaned out and knocked on his doorframe. The door was still propped open, and I took another step, peering inside. Trey was there, along with another guy. I waved at them, and smiled but then stepped back, hoping Trey would come to me, which he did.

He came into the hallway quickly, looking me over. His smile faded so quickly that my heart dropped. He was staring straight at my eyes, or the side of my face. He was definitely staring cautiously.

"What happened to you, Tara?"

"What is it?" I asked, leaning back as he came toward me.

He stared intensely at the side of my face. "Who did this to you?" he asked. "You have a black eye."

He was so upset about it that I turned and walked the few steps back to my apartment so that I could look in the mirror. I had no idea what he was talking about. I hadn't been hit at practice and no one said anything about me having a black eye. I hadn't stared at myself or anything, but I glanced in the mirror when I took a shower, and I didn't see it.

I went to my apartment, and Trey followed me. There was a mirror in my entryway, and I stared into it, focusing on the side of my face where he had been staring.

"Oh that?" I said. "That's not a black eye. It's just a little burn. Like a carpet burn or whatever—a brush burn." I tilted my face to the side staring at the small red patch near the corner of my right eye. "Something just rubbed me right there. It's probably from his glove, or even his hair or beard."

"Whose hair or beard?"

"Miguel's."

"Your boyfriend?"

I laughed. "No. He's… he's seventeen. He boxes at my dad's gym. He's really good. He's only been training for about six months, but he's already going to take an amateur match."

"I don't understand how he has a beard at seventeen or how he was rubbing it on you."

"It's not a full beard. It's just that any little facial hair can rub you the wrong way if someone's chin bumps you. He wasn't rubbing it on me, but boxing is a contact sport. Something just rubbed me right there. It happens all the time. It'll fade in a day or two. In a match, you would put lubricant on your face to prevent that."

"Are you a boxer?" he asked.

"I train, and I help some of the fighters train, but I don't compete."

I held onto the towel, taking a step back from him, so that we could talk. "I didn't mean to break up your meeting but I got your note."

"Is your dad okay with you boxing with guys even when you get hurt like this?" he asked.

I smiled at him for being so concerned. "It must look worse than it is," I said gesturing to it. "This is no big deal at all. Yes, my dad knows I'm boxing with guys. I'm one of Miguel's main training partners. He'll outgrow me soon, but for now, we're good for each other."

He stared at me for a good, long while before he spoke again. "Well, about the note, I was just looking at the measurements of this place, and it seems like I am missing some space upstairs. Did Stan ever say anything about a closet or hidden room?"

"Hidden room?" I said. "Like where you pull a book and the shelf opens up? I wish I had one of those in my apartment."

"Something like that," Trey said. "But it seems like it would be back here on this end of the building. I was wondering if Stan ever mentioned it."

"No," I said. "We weren't that close, though."

"Okay," Trey said, nodding. "Hey, if I wanted to have dinner somewhere besides Carson's, where do you think I should go? Elliot's? The seafood place, is that place any good?"

"Elliot's, no, definitely not. Don't go there. Go to Miller's. Elliot's is terrible."

"Oh, wow. I'm glad I asked."

"Did you not want to say anything about my rent?" I said. "I thought that's what the note was about. I thought maybe you decided on a price. I'm really waiting to hear what you say on that."

"Oh, no. I hadn't thought about it," he said. "When is your lease up? Six months?"

"Three months," I said.

He shook his head. "I've got it in your file. I'll have to look at it. I've just got so much going on. I'm looking at another building on Market Street."

"What do you mean you're looking at it?"

"I'm looking at it to buy," he said.

I tilted my head. "Really? Why?"

Trey tilted his head back at me. A piece of his hair fell over his forehead when he did it, and he used his hand to push it back. He was a lady killer, but I was too distracted by my uncertain future to care.

"Because I think it's a good investment. I have this place now, and I like this city. I'll be coming back to check on this building, anyway, I might as well have another one. The one on Market street is three story, but it's smaller than this one square-footage-wise. It's got a storefront and four apartments, two on each floor. But everything's smaller. If I end up keeping an apartment vacant for myself in Galveston, it'll probably be one of those because they're smaller than these."

"Maybe I can move into one of your smaller ones. Are they nice? I'm sorry. I didn't realize what a good deal we were getting at this place," I said. "It's my first time to be on my own, so even this seemed like a lot of money to me." I backed away from him slowly, going to hang my towel on the back of a chair. I looked at him and continued what I was saying. "I went to a few other places, and I realized you were right, this place is worth more than I'm paying."

"You tried to move out?" he asked.

"I wouldn't say I tried, not just yet, but I'm looking for another place, sure. I went to a few apartments, just to see what my price range could get me."

"You didn't tell me you were looking at other places," he said.

I smiled. "Would it matter?" I asked. "You had to know I'm thinking about that. I mean, look at Stan. He's here today and gone tomorrow."

"I told you I'd work with you."

"Why would you do that for me and not him?" I asked.

He stared at me with an unreadable expression. "I don't know. Because I like you more than I like him. Because I feel like it. I'm not sure. Does it matter?"

"No," I said. There was a long pause, and I stared at Trey. I needed to have some concrete information. I was tired of everything being up in the air. "In three months, when my lease is up, I'd like to sign another one. One more year of living here. Please. I'll pay fifty dollars a month more than I'm paying now. It's not a lot, but I can't go higher than that. I could do some work around here if it'll help you. That will give me one more year to figure things out with trying to start a business. I feel like I'll know more about where my life is going by then. Or maybe I won't, but three months is going to be here before I know it, and I hate to leave that soon. I can move back in with my parents if it comes to that, but if you could find it in your heart to agree to one more—"

"Sure," Trey said.

I paused.

"Sure?"

"Yes."

"You agree to what I just said?" I asked, whispering.

My door was open, and I didn't want my neighbors to hear since I was certain this deal didn't apply to everyone.

"I'll let you sign another year," he said, nodding.

"With only raising the rent fifty dollars?" I whispered, wide-eyed.

"Yes," he said, whispering back in an exaggerated tone. *Was he teasing me?* For a moment, things were light and easy, and I felt like he was my friend. I was happy. It felt like an actual weight had been lifted off my shoulders with the news of a new lease.

It felt so good to know I had a plan for another year. I reached in and gave him a tight hug, and then I stuck my arm out stiffly, staring at him and waiting for a handshake.

Trey grinned at me, but he reached out and shook my hand. I wanted to hug him again. I wanted to ask him to dinner since he had mentioned trying to find a restaurant. It was one of those times when I wanted to go overboard and try to be best buddies with him, but I had to stop myself. I just bowed humbly. "Thank you so much," I said. "Really. If you need me to do anything for you, you know, as far as the building, just ask. I'm here all the time, and I'd be happy to keep an eye on the place for you."

"Thank you," he said.

***

"Could it really be that easy?" I asked my mom the following day. It was Sunday, and I was eating lunch at my parents' house after church.

"Could what be that easy?" Mom asked.

My brother walked up beside her and she held out a bite of the chicken that she was deboning.

"For the last month, I've seen this guy as my enemy. I was bummed out about moving, and I just saw him as the guy who was kicking me out. I had crazy thoughts about him that I would never act

61

on—stuff like maybe I should vandalize the place so that he thinks bad of it and wants to sell it."

My mother scowled at me. "Tara Grace!"

"I'd never do it, Mom. I'm just saying… I thought of him as the enemy, and now that's all changed. He says he's not doubling my rent, and suddenly I want to sweep the staircase and take him to dinner."

"Take him to dinner?" Will said, playing the role of the concerned male since my father was outside.

"Not like that, Will. I'm just saying. It's amazing how one conversation can make you go from someone's enemy to someone's friend.

"God told me something about enemies years ago," my mom said. "One place in the Bible, it says that *love keeps no record of wrong* and then in another place in the Bible it says to *love your enemy*. And then one day, I just had this thought. Okay, let me see if I can say it right… A record of wrong is all I have on my enemies, right? They're only enemies *because* of the record of wrong that I keep. So, if I get rid of that record of wrongs, like the Bible tells me to, then they're not enemies anymore. If it tells me to love my enemy and then tells me love keeps no record of wrong, then that means I have no enemies."

There were a few seconds of silence.

"That's deep, Mom," Will said.

"It is deep," she said, nodding at him. She looked at me. "It's a little different in your case. This guy gave you a gift, and so forgiving him was made easy."

"But theoretically, I shouldn't have been mad at him in the first place. Is that what you're saying?"

"Yeah, I'm not saying that there won't be conflict in your life or that you need to let people walk all over you, but there's something to be said for not making enemies, even in your own mind. There's something to be said for forgiving people and moving on with your thoughts."

"Well, thankfully Trey did make it easy for me, like you said. He's being really kind about it. I can't believe all I had to do was ask."

"What's he going to do with Stan's old apartment?" Mom asked. "I might know somebody who's interested. My hairdresser's sister is going through a divorce."

I shook my head and shrugged. "I'll ask him when he thinks it'll be ready."

Chapter 7

The door to apartment 202 was open when I came home later that afternoon. I peeked inside, wondering if I could see any changes or construction. Trey was all the way across the room, so I just smiled at him and kept walking. I was in the process of unlocking my door when I heard footsteps approaching.

"Oh, hi," I said when I turned and saw Trey in the hall. He had on jeans and an old t-shirt. I could see why Jesse had reacted to him on that first day. He was such a nice-looking guy. I had been so worried about my fate that I hadn't noticed. Now that I didn't see Trey as a threat, I could finally see him objectively. I glanced downward when I had the thought. I instinctually adjusted my hair and then reached back and put my hand on the door handle, but didn't open it.

"I wanted to let you know that my mom might know someone who wants to rent 202 from you when you're ready. She was asking me about it." I was holding a bowl of food so I gestured to the apartment behind him with a flick of my chin.

I saw him look at my bowl.

"It's chicken," I said. "It's leftovers from my mom's house from lunch today. My dad barbecued chicken, and we... this is just a bunch of pulled chicken, you know for sandwiches or whatever. I might make chicken salad with it tomorrow, once I'm tired of eating it like this." I had no idea why I was over-sharing. Maybe I was nervous around him now because I felt indebted about the rent. "I have plenty if you want some," I added, to my own disbelief. The offer just came out of my mouth before I could have second thoughts about it.

"I'm actually starving," he said, touching his stomach. "I ate a big breakfast this morning, and I ended up skipping lunch."

"Oh, you want some of this?"

I must have sounded surprised because he said, "Weren't you offering?"

"Yes, I was, but I didn't think you'd say 'yes'."

He laughed at that.

"I didn't think you'd want leftovers. But you can have some." And then I remembered how much of a discount he was giving me on the rent and I stuck out my hand, balancing the bowl in the air between us. "You can have it all, actually." It was heavy, and it teetered, so I took my other hand off of the doorknob to support it, still holding it out for him to take.

He just stared at it. "I'm not going to take all of your food."

"Oh, really, it's fine," I said, holding it out, insisting.

He took it from me reluctantly. "This is heavy," he said. "What's in here? Just chicken?"

"Yeah, it's a bunch of pulled chicken. Barbecue."

"There must be at least a whole chicken in here."

"Oh, at least. My dad grilled six of them, and some sausages, too. We all eat it for leftovers."

"Well, I don't want you to give me the whole thing. Can I just make a sandwich out of it and give you the rest?"

"Sure," I said taking it back and realizing it was probably kind of weird of me to give him that much chicken. "I just wanted you to do what you wanted. You know, like if you wanted it for leftovers tomorrow or whatever. I didn't know how long you were staying in Galveston."

"A few more days," he said.

"Are you going to rent it out after that? The apartment? Because my mom knows someone who might be looking." I motioned for him to follow me, and we went inside. "I can put a little of this in a bowl for you to make your own sandwich, or I can make you one here. All I have is wheat bread. I might have some pita bread, too."

I glanced over my shoulder at him, and he smiled. "All I have is no bread. I'll take either of those you mentioned. I was about to go out for dinner, but I'd just as soon stay here. I'm up to my ears exploring this building."

Trey followed me into my kitchen. He leaned against the cabinet while I went to work putting a few things away and making him a barbecue chicken sandwich.

I loved food, and I did for him what I would have done for myself (except double the portion). I made him a chicken sandwich with just the right proportion of meat to bread. I heated it evenly and carefully cut it in half. I added a handful of regular potato chips and a pickle spear from the fridge. I did all of this while we continued our conversation.

"Nobody's working today, since it's Sunday, so it's been quiet around here. I have a few people coming to give estimates tomorrow and the next day. And I'm going to tour that place on Market Street."

"Where on Market Street is it?" I asked.

"It's near 25th. It's the pink building next to the Italian restaurant."

"You're kidding. That's a cool building. The candle store?"

"I think that's what was down there. But they're moving."

"I pass that building all the time." I imagined the candle store, and tried to think about if it would be large enough for a studio. That candle store was quite a bit smaller than the jewelry store, but I thought maybe I could make it work for a studio if the rent was a lot cheaper. "I didn't even know it was for sale," I said.

"It's not on the market yet. Justin knows about it from another one of his clients. He's the one who told me about it."

"That might not be a bad spot for me," I said. "Depending on how big it is." I slid the plate in front of Trey, and he thanked me.

"You're welcome. I hope you like it. You can sit here or take it back with you. Either way, I'm gonna go put my things away."

"I'll stay here and eat if you don't mind," he said.

"Okay, I'll come back in just a second, then."

I started to take off, but I thought of getting him a glass of water since he was staying. Quickly, I took a glass from the cabinet, filled with water, and set it in front of Trey.

I smiled at him as I walked out of the kitchen. He thanked me again, and I went into my room, feeling like I was vulnerable to his gaze. I assumed he was looking at me from behind, and for some reason, I cared. I didn't know how to feel about my reaction to Trey. I hadn't expected to offer him a plate of food or for him to accept it and sit there and eat in my kitchen.

I thought about what my mom said about enemies. I remembered her saying it was easy for me to like Trey since he had done me a favor. I felt like I wanted to impress him now, and I figured I was only acting that way because he had helped me out. I tried to make myself feel guilty for wanting to make myself look presentable, but I still went to do it.

I left Trey in the kitchen to eat by himself while I went into my bedroom. I regarded my reflection in the mirror. I had on a skirt from this morning, and my dark hair was styled in an easy up style similar to a French twist. I was comfortable, but I took my hair down and changed into a pair of overall shorts with a t-shirt.

I turned upside down and shook my hair out, causing it to fall in a tangled mass of black waves over my shoulders. I ran my fingers through it, strategically taming it down. I thought about powdering my nose, or spraying some perfume, but I thought that would be too much. I reminded myself that he had already agreed on the contract, and even shook on it.

I did not need to impress this man. I repeated that to myself, even as I tucked and straightened and checked myself. I went back into the kitchen only a few minutes after I went into my bedroom.

"That was fast," he said, glancing at me when he heard me coming. "You changed and everything."

I smiled at him. He was just about done with his whole plate of food. "I was ready to get comfortable," I said. "I'm glad you liked your sandwich."

"I loved it," he said. "It was really good. Thank you for making me that."

"You're welcome," I said. "The same thing is on the menu tomorrow. Maybe I'll add eggs and mayonnaise and make a chicken salad... if you're not sick of chicken by then."

"I won't be," he said. "I'd love some more of this."

I had been mostly joking—making fun of myself for eating leftovers for days. But he seemed to be taking it as a serious offer.

"Some more right now, or some other time?"

"No, I'm good right now."

"I have plenty if you seriously want more of it," I said. "I could give you some in a bowl to take with you right now, or I'll make you another sandwich whenever you're ready."

"I'll take another one at ten o'clock tonight," he said.

"Really?"

He grinned. "No. I would never ask you to do that. I do eat snacks at that time of night. I'm sure I'll be pouring a bowl of cereal or something. I went to the store yesterday and got a few groceries and a microwave."

"Oh, for this apartment?" I asked, gesturing behind him.

"Yeah. It was cheaper for me to get a few supplies for this place than it was to get a hotel. And I'd rather be here to see what I want to do with the building."

"Where are you going to sleep? Is there a bed in there?"

"Back in the day, these apartments were rented furnished," he said. "Apparently Stan's bedframe was left over from that, because he left a note saying it wasn't his. All I had to do was buy a box spring and mattress. It's just a little twin… my feet basically hang off the end." He laughed and then added, "Even with that, and the rest of the stuff I bought, it was cheaper than a hotel would have been."

"I could always stay with my parents if you want to stay in my place for a few nights," I offered.

Trey turned to me quickly and regarded me with a curious stare as if he didn't know how to take my offer.

I shrugged. "It is your building. I just feel like I owe you with what a good deal you're giving me on the rent."

"I'm raising your rent by fifty dollars," he said.

"When you could be doing it by a lot more."

"You don't need to thank me," he said. "This whole building is a gift. I'm still finding new things about it. It's amazing. I don't know what kind of man my great-grandfather was, but this building is crazy.

"Was it your great-grandfather who built it?"

"No. But I think he made a bunch of changes to it. I'm trying to put the pieces together. I have very little information on him. Something happened between my grandfather and his parents that made him not talk about it. They had money and they were crazy, that's all I knew. My grandfather and my dad and his siblings, they all got nothing from the will when Joan died. But me and my siblings and all ten of my cousins got money. They got just over a hundred grand each. I got the building, and I assumed, based on my family's attitude, that I got the short end of the stick. For the last two years, I've been thinking I was lucky to have renters at all. More than once, I wished she would have given me the money like she did with my cousins."

"But now you like it here?" I asked.

He nodded dazedly. "It's hand's down the coolest thing I've ever been given," he said. "Todd and Justin… they've been digging for me, trying to find out all they can. As far as I could tell, my great-grandfather, Frank, and Joan opened a book store in the early forties and ran it for a little over a decade until he died, and that's when the jeweler moved in. Joan stayed single in the upstairs apartment. No one even knew they had kids or grandkids. That's all of the story that Justin knew."

"You might not ever know any more than that," I said. "My dad had a bunch of stuff happen with his parents. My mom said some of it's so bad they'll probably never tell me about it. She said that some things are just better left unsaid."

"Is your dad good to you in spite of that stuff?" he asked.

"Of course. He's amazing. He's the kindest, most protective father. He's been nothing but a champion for me my whole life—and he has plenty of family issues—past stuff. Things happen to people sometimes. People carry baggage we don't even know about."

Chapter 8

I spent the next few hours with Trey.

After he ate his chicken sandwich, he asked if I wanted to go to the beach. I agreed to go, and we went out walking on the seawall until the sun began to go down. He was smart and funny, and we shared effortless conversation. It was easy liking him now that the landlord-tenant thing was out of the equation. There was no strain.

I had fun talking to Trey. I played tour guide, showing him a few of the good spots that only locals knew about. I intentionally led us to his truck as the sun began getting lower in the sky.

Trey was driving, but I told him where to go.

I took him on a long loop to get back to the apartment, showing him a few of my favorite restaurants and stores on our way back. Finally, we made our way home. He parked on Bank Street, in front of the hardware store, only a few feet from the door to the apartment.

Neither of us hesitated, and we walked up the stairs, having casual conversation like we had done all afternoon.

"Hey, thank you, Tara," he said from behind me as we went up the staircase.

"You're welcome. I had fun."

"I want to go back and play some of those games on the boardwalk," he said.

"Which one?" I asked.

"Land the ball in the basket," Trey said.

I smiled at him and shook my head as I made it to the top of the stairs. "That one's impossible," I said. "That's why the prizes are so big. The bigger the prize, the more impossible the game."

"Like they always say," Trey said with an amused grin.

I was charmed by him, and the realization of that made me take a step away. "Okay, I'll see ya," I said.

I waved and smiled as I began retreating down the hall toward my apartment.

"Oh, Tara, I wasn't going to show anybody this, and now you've got me wanting to so bad..." Trey gazed at me thoughtfully like he was really contemplating something.

"What are you talking about?" I asked.

"I found a secret in this building, and I promised myself I would tell no one on this earth about it, and now I just keep wanting to show you."

"Oh, now you've got me curious. Now you can't *not* show me."

"Do you want to see it?" he asked.

"Yes!" I said with wide eyes even though I had no idea what it was. My first thought was that he had found treasure buried in the wall or a floorboard—like a treasure map or the original copy of the Declaration of Independence.

"Is it treasure?" I asked.

He let out a little laugh. "No. Kind of, but no. Come on."

As he told me to come on, he reached out and grabbed my hand to pull me along. He let go of me as soon as he touched me, but there had been contact, and I was hyper aware of it.

"Where are we going?" I asked. I fell into stride behind him, following him back down the stairs. My heart was pounding by the time we reached the bottom.

"It's next door," he said, even though I had a hunch already.

I followed Trey along the sidewalk for several paces until we reached the door to the jewelry store. He unlocked it and glanced around before he went inside. He locked the door behind us and took off, heading toward the back.

"Okay, so back here in the hallway on the way to the office, there's a big linen closet. I don't know if you remember that, but—"

"I do," I said. I had taken pictures and I knew the building well. I knew there were a few nice closets in the hall.

"Oh, whoa, what happened?" I said, seeing the mess that had been made as we walked past the front room and deeper into the building.

There was a stack of wood and drywall in the hall where the closet had been demolished, leaving a small, empty compartment that was roughly three feet square.

Debris was stacked in the hallway, and I got caught up staring at it, but Trey got my attention by opening the door the rest of the way and stepping into the closet.

"First, I noticed this spackle peeling back at the seam right here," he said. "And then I saw that there was a piece of metal in the wall. It looked like there were gears, and I was like why would there be gears?" He pointed up, and I glanced that way. I could see where the wall had been peeled back exposing a big metal mechanism in the wall near the ceiling.

"I'm sure there was a switch at one point," he said. "My guess was that there was a shelf facing this way," he gestured to the side wall where the machine parts had been revealed. "Like maybe you pull a certain book off the shelf and it triggers a secret passage, like you were saying."

At first, I thought he had been messing with me, and then I realized, based on the destruction, that he might be serious. I widened my eyes at him, pointing at the closet. "Is this a secret passage?" I asked.

He nodded excitedly. "I found the switch in the wall, but the shelves were still in at that point. I tried to flip the switch, but they were in the way. It wouldn't work. You'll see. You'll see how it works. I was in here all morning. I noticed that metal yesterday, and I just couldn't stop thinking about it. I had to peel back this wall to figure it out, and then it wouldn't work with the shelves. You'll see. You have to be inside."

"Be inside?"

"Yes. Come here."

He stepped to one side of the closet offering me a little room on the other side. I stepped in cautiously, feeling ridiculously close to him. He was tall and broad, and hard-bodied, and I was only noticing those things because I was basically pressed up against him.

"Just trust me," he said reassuringly. "You have to be all the way inside, and the door has to be closed."

He held me close, pulling me near. I started to get a thrill from it, but then I realized he was only doing it to use me for leverage. He closed the pocket door, making it dark inside, and then he reached up and pulled a lever.

"Sorry, it's only going to be dark for a second. It won't work unless this door is closed." Suddenly, I heard a low, humming, mechanical noise. I pulled back and looked at him with wide eyes.

"Just a second," he assured me, smiling.

It was dark, but I could see enough to see him smile. I just stood there being quiet while things began to move. I reached out and held onto his arm, feeling a little scared and starting to wonder what I had gotten myself into.

Trey gave me a few compassionate pats on my arm. "Trust me," he said. "I wouldn't let you get hurt. This door needs oil. I think it's supposed to go quicker."

I had no idea what he was talking about. We were completely surrounded on all four sides, but I still trusted him. I glanced up at him, but I could barely make out the outlines of his face. I thought he might use the few seconds of mysterious darkness to kiss me, but he didn't. I got all woozy and melty at the thought. I was still staring upward at him as the back wall opened slowly.

"Oh my gosh, this is insane! Is there another room over there?"

He held onto me. "Just stand here for a second and let it open. It takes a few seconds."

I stayed still for several long seconds as the wall opened up.

"I thought we were going to be glued into the wall for a second there," I said, sounding relieved.

He laughed. "You thought I was gluing you into the wall? You sure did give in easily if you thought that's what was going on here."

"Well, obviously I trust you if I'm not fighting. But if you were really trying to glue me into the wall, you better believe I would fight."

I stared at the back wall as it continued to open, revealing another tiny room on the other side. It was mostly dark still, but I could see that there was another space there.

"Is this a secret closet?" I asked, peering into it.

"Yeah. And it's extremely secret. I have the blueprints for this place, and none of this exists. Todd and Justin don't know about it. No one does. Todd mentioned something being off with the measurements, but I haven't let them get close enough to figure this out."

"Oh, gosh, it's a staircase," I said, when the back wall finally opened completely and I could see the tiny room on the other side. The only place to go was up a small spiral staircase. It was dimly lit, but I could see a little. The steps were iron, and the stairway was lined in gorgeous wood paneling. The wood walls were a stark contrast to the closet where we stood, which had been torn up by Trey ripping the shelves out and tearing the drywall down.

I stepped onto the first step of the spiral staircase, but I turned and looked back at Trey. I figured it'd be better to ask if he wanted to go first since he knew where he was going. I turned as he came to stand behind me, and I found that we were eye to eye. "Wow, how tall are you?" I asked, saying the first thing that came to my mind.

"Six-two."

"Oh, really? I didn't realize."

I leaned back when I noticed how close we were.

"Did you want to go first?" I asked.

There was only room for one of us on that staircase, so we would have to switch places if he wanted to go up first, but I had no idea where I was going.

"There's only one place to go," he said. "There's one room at the top, and I left a night light plugged in earlier, so you should be able to see once you get up there."

I nodded and turned, trying not to notice that Trey had been incredibly close to me. He wasn't brushing up against me or anything, but it was a tight space, and we were close. I did my best to ignore his presence, but I was aware of Trey Harper in a different way now.

My eyes had adjusted to the darkness, and I easily climbed the steps.

"It's wired for lights, but the bulbs are out, and it takes a special kind of bulb."

The staircase turned and opened up, and I gasped at the gorgeous little room that was waiting at the top of the steps.

"Where in the world am I?" I said dazedly, dramatically.

"I left a flashlight there at the top of the stairs," he said from behind me.

I continued to climb until I reached the top of the steps. I found myself in a much larger room than I ever expected. It wasn't gigantic, but it was maybe twelve-by-twelve. I knew it was somewhere close to that because I knew how to estimate after considering different studio spaces.

Two walls were covered in built in bookshelves, but they were empty now. I was too busy looking around to worry about the flashlight, but Trey grabbed it when he made his way into the room. Things got brighter when he turned it on.

It was a green room with wooden built-in bookshelves on two sides. The shelves were made of thick wood and had intricate details.

"There were a few books on the top shelves," Trey said, "about fifty of them. They might be valuable. They're antiques, first editions. I took them down to the apartment to check them out. I was looking at them up here, but it's dark, and it's dusty. I was getting allergies. I had just finished hauling them down when I ran into you and you made me the sandwich. I needed a break from all this, anyway. It was overwhelming."

"You had to go down with them, and then outside and back up to the apartment?" I asked, imagining him hauling books.

"Yes," he said with a chuckle. He gently knocked on the wall to his right. "I'm pretty sure if I put a hole in this wall, I'd be standing in my apartment, but yes, I had to go all the way down and around."

I noticed that he referred to 202 as *his* apartment, but I didn't say anything about it since technically the whole building was his.

"This room is unbelievable," I said, looking all around. "I cannot believe we just went through the back of the closet. Where are we, even? I mean, I know we're upstairs, but you think we're next to 202?" I reached out and put my hand on the wall he had touched, as if that would help me get my bearings.

"My guess is that we're between apartment 202 and 203. Maybe the supply closet is here," he said, pointing. "But there's no way into either of them from this room. Not that I can tell, at least, and I poked and prodded around in here for over an hour earlier."

There was a sliding ladder on the bookshelf, and he pointed the flashlight toward the top of it. "This ladder looks like it goes to another exit, though." He used the flashlight to aim at the ceiling. "My guess is that this frame in the ceiling is a window onto the roof—a hatch or whatever—an exit route, if you needed it. I've got to have some work done to restore this, but it would be amazing to have a skylight there."

"So, there's a top-secret room that leads up to the roof? Plus, you found a bunch of valuable books? That's all you've been doing with your day before we hung out? How uneventful! You must be so bored."

I was being sarcastic, and he smiled, and nodded, knowing how amazing this was.

"I can't believe this is here and none of the people in the apartments ever even knew about it," I said. "I wonder if Mister McCain knew."

"No. Nobody knows about it," he said. "And I like it that way. Todd would figure it out if he came in here, and I don't want him to. He already mentioned there being lost space on the second floor. I think I'm just going to hire his crew to do the bathrooms and kitchens and hire other people to do the rest. I figured I can keep it a mystery if I hire two different crews, one to work on the sky light restoration from the roof, and one to fix up the closet and trap door from downstairs. I'll do some of it myself. I'm going to board the closet up for now and tell my contractors to stay out of here."

"Are you trying to keep people from knowing this room exists?" I asked, feeling a little confused.

"Yes, I am," he said. "I don't want to tell a soul about it, so please don't mention it—not even to construction workers. It's fun to have something no one else knows about. That's why it's a secret passage. Because no one knows about it."

"Yeah, but I know about it," I said.

Trey stared at me, blinking a couple of times like he was thinking. "I know, but you're different. I don't want those guys to know—or anyone else."

I looked around, glancing up, taking it all in. I could've imagined the window being open and functioning. It would've been magical. It already was magical.

"Thank you for sharing this with me," I said.

"You're welcome."

I smiled at him. "Should I be scared the door might get stuck and we'll be in here forever?"

Oh, gosh. Was I flirting? Stop.

"No. We're not stuck. All we have to do is knock a hole in one of these walls and we'll be in my apartment. In fact, I thought about making another door into here from there while I'm doing renovations. That way I could reach this room from my apartment or downstairs. If I end up renting this place out to anyone but you, I'll probably make the downstairs entrance unusable like it was." He shrugged. "I'd almost rather no one use it at all if it's not you."

"It'll always be me," I said.

He chuckled at that. "I'm still trying to comprehend that this room even exists. My guess is that no one's been up here for years. I guess Joan Harper could have known about it at one point, but she never left any clues. Maybe she was the one who boarded it up and built the shelves."

I bent down and got on the floor slowly, first to my knees and then I turned and laid on my back. I sprawled out in the center of the room, staring up at the ceiling. The wood floors were dusty, but I didn't care, I could imagine this place in its full splendor with sun shining down through a window in the roof. I imagined a seating area with chairs and a table and some plants. It would have been really glorious with these shelves all cleaned up and full of books.

Trey and I stayed up there and talked for an hour or so. He loved this new secret room, and I couldn't blame him. I loved it, too. I had never seen anything like it. It was hidden, secret, special. I could tell he didn't want anyone else to know about it, and I didn't plan on telling. His secret was safe with me. I had no idea why he shared it with me, but I was glad, and I didn't plan on betraying his trust.

Chapter 9

Trey
Ten o'clock that evening

Trey had no idea why he told Tara about the secret room. The minute he found it, he assured himself that he wasn't going to tell a soul, and before the end of the day, he had already taken Tara up there. Trey normally didn't have a problem with breaking his own resolve. He was a private person who had never felt the need to share information with people before he was ready.

He had a whole plan about hiring different crews to work on different parts of the room so that no one knew the full scope of the hidden treasure from rooftop to closet. Trey was a smart guy who had figured out a way to get the secret room restored while still keeping the full experience a secret.

And then, Tara Castro was about to say goodnight to him, and he just couldn't take it. He marched her downstairs and proceeded to show her the entire thing, bottom to top. He even told her about the books. There wasn't a single detail that he kept from her.

He would've normally been mad at himself for doing something like that, but honestly, in this case, he would do it again. He liked Tara, and he had no regrets. They stayed upstairs, talking for a while after he showed it to her, and she had some great ideas about fixing it up and making it beautiful again.

It was 9pm when they said goodnight, and Tara knocked on his door an hour later.

He opened the door, smiling when he saw that it was her. He immediately noticed that she was holding a plate. It was covered with a paper napkin, so he couldn't see what was on it, but he assumed it was a chicken sandwich.

"I was in the kitchen and it was ten o'clock, so I thought I'd make you another one. You know, since you said that about ten o'clock. You don't have to eat it if you don't—"

"I want it so much," Trey said. "I'm hungry. It's perfect timing."

She smiled. "I made a plate with chips and a pickle, like before."

Tara was bold and fearless, she had a scratch on her eye from boxing with a guy. And yet she smiled at Trey, and acted all proper, holding out the plate like she was shy to offer it to him. She was utterly irresistible. Trey wanted to pull her into his arms and kiss her—to claim her. He grinned, ignoring the urge as he took the plate from her.

"I don't want you to regret telling me," she whispered. "I really won't tell anyone. I'll forget you told me."

"Don't forget," Trey insisted easily. "That'd be a shame if you forgot."

She looked up and stared at him. Both of their hands were on the plate, and she let go of it once she realized Trey had a hold of it.

"It's awesome that you really brought this," he said. "I was thinking about that conversation, and it crossed my mind that you might."

She smiled and shrugged. "When you have chicken for days, sometimes you have to share with neighbors."

Trey grinned as he cut his eyes toward apartment 203, making sure the neighbors were nowhere in sight before looking back at her. "Come here for a second, I want to tell you something." He was whispering, acting like he didn't want them to be overheard, but really, he just wanted Tara to come closer. There was no one around, but she came near to him, offering him her ear so that he could say what he wanted to say.

"Thank you," he whispered. He spoke slowly, intentionally trying to hold her there. They were ever so close, and the air between them was absolutely charged. The tension was tangible. You could cut it with a knife.

Tara put her mouth closer to his ear. "You're welcome," she whispered slowly. She started to step back, but Trey reached in and kissed her cheek. Tara hesitated there, letting it happen.

It was just a kiss on the cheek, but Trey's body was alive with anticipation. Her skin was like velvet, soft and warm. He loved that she stood there and let his mouth touch her skin, even if it was only for a few seconds. She moved. She touched his arm, and it seemed like she was going to turn and kiss him on the mouth... but just then, there was unexpected noise.

Tara jumped back instantly, and it was a good thing she did, because the door to the back apartment opened, and Charlotte and Mickey showed up in the doorway of it. Tara and Trey barely had any warning at all. The sound of the door handle was all that happened before the other couple showed up in the common area.

"Oh, hey, y'all," Tara said, stepping back. "And, thanks Mister Harper, I just had that one question for you," she said, continuing a nonexistent conversation with Trey. "Thank you for answering it. I'll try that with the thermostat next time. Night everyone," she added, waving at Charlotte and Mickey and then at Trey.

She took off, making her way back to her own apartment so fast that Trey didn't know what hit him.

They had been just about to kiss.

He wanted to kiss her so badly.

How in the world was the opportunity over? It seemed impossible that it was over.

Mickey said something to Trey, and Trey answered, but he was totally preoccupied with his encounter with Tara—his time with her. He had just spent the whole evening with the person who was quickly becoming the woman of his dreams. His chest actually ached when he thought about how close they had been to kissing when they were interrupted just now.

He wanted to rush back over to her apartment.

But he didn't.

He ate his sandwich and went to sleep thinking about her. The following day was Monday, and for Trey, it would be a busy one. He got up at 6am and visited the hardware store where he got supplies to clean that closet.

He had some cleanup to do from the day before, and he barely got things done before his meeting with Todd Benson. They talked about pulling out the cabinets and refinishing the trim and the floors.

Todd asked about the offices and closets, but Trey told him he was getting to that area later, and that was a good enough explanation. Trey ate lunch with Todd after they took some measurements. They talked about the pink building, and one other investment property, and then at 1pm, Trey went to Bank Street Boxing for a workout.

He wasn't doing it just to try to run into Tara. He would love to run into her, but this visit was scheduled before they had gotten close. Trey set up a tour and trial lesson two weeks ago, and it was happening today.

He was told it would be with a man named Dizzy, but it was none other than Easy Billy Castro who came around the corner after Trey checked in. Trey stood up to shake Billy's hand when he saw him coming that way.

"Billy Castro," he said, introducing himself with a firm handshake.

"Trey Harper. I'm Billy, too. William, technically. William the third. That's where Trey comes from."

"Should I call you Trey?" Billy asked.

Trey was nervous around him. He told himself that it was because Billy was a famous boxer, but the truth was it was that he was Tara's dad. Trey felt like Billy could see right through him, like he knew he was in love with his daughter the instant they shook hands.

"Trey's great," he said. "Yes sir, you can call me... I'm Trey. That's all I've ever gone by."

"I'm Billy."

"I know your daughter," Trey said.

"I know."

"You do? Did she say something about me?" Trey realized he wasn't being casual enough and he added. "I'm afraid landlords have to be the bad guy sometimes."

"I don't know what you mean by that. My daughter didn't seem to think you are a bad guy."

"Oh no, I'm, I just didn't know, you know because I, she might have told you I was raising the rent."

This conversation happened as they walked across the gym, but it faded out as they came to the side of the ring. For the next hour, Billy gave Trey the rundown on the sport and the gym. He told him it's a good sport to practice to stay physically fit and learn how to defend yourself even if you don't plan on doing it professionally.

They toured the gym, and then Billy went to the wall where extra gloves and pads were stored. Billy suited Trey up with boxing gloves, and he, himself, strapped on thick pads—the ones used to catch a boxer's punches.

Billy put Trey through a fast-paced workout where he made him do alternating reps of conditioning drills and boxing. He would call out combinations so fast that Trey couldn't keep up. Trey knew a little about boxing, but he was overwhelmed by all the new information and the speed at which it was being thrown at him.

Trey was in the middle of doing a basic *jab, cross, hook* combination when Tara walked through the door.

She took his breath away.

She was wearing those dang shorts and a loose-fitting shirt that hung off of one shoulder.

"Jab, jab, cross, hook to the body," Billy said, but it sounded like unintelligible babbling in the background of the Tara show. And...

Slap.

That thick pad came out faster than lightning and tagged Trey on the side of the head, getting his attention off of Tara.

"Jab, jab, cross, hook to the body," Billy repeated.

Trey performed the sequence of punches, several times in a row, resetting between each set. He tried to do his best, punching smoothly and cleanly in case Tara looked his way. He thought about almost kissing her, and he delivered the next combination with more power than before.

"Relax," Billy said.

"I'm sorry," Trey said.

He glanced at Tara again, and she was looking at him. She smiled and waved, and Trey smiled back at her since he was not about to wave in front of her dad and with a big boxing glove.

"Pay attention," Billy said.

"Cross, hook, cross, and then drop and do two hooks to the body. We're gonna do it five times, reset each time, go."

Trey did the combination Billy called for, slowly at first, making sure he got the order correct. By the end, he knew he was doing it right. He felt strong, like it went well. He could not stop himself from glancing Tara's way as the round finished. He sought her approval, and he hoped she had been watching that.

"What are you looking at?" Billy said.

"Y-your daughter, sir," Trey hated to admit it, but he knew there was no point in lying since it was obvious.

"Why are you looking at my daughter?" Billy asked, as if it was a serious question and he was genuinely wondering.

Trey spoke hesitantly when he said, "B-because she's amazing."

Billy Castro lunged forward and threw a stiff jab, straight into Trey Harper's jaw. He used the edge of the pad, and it extended a little farther than he anticipated. He hit Trey with a jab that would have, quite frankly, knocked some men out. Billy intended it as a warning tag for saying such a thing, but he hit the guy hard. Billy could tell by the way Trey's head snapped back.

Billy was at close range, and he was a world champion. Trey had no idea what happened. He saw stars and heard ringing, and then Billy's face came into focus.

"I meant to tap you, but you moved," Billy said. "You probably got your bell rung a little bit."

"Yeah," Trey said.

He felt a surge of adrenaline, and he desperately wanted to hit Billy back. He stopped himself. Not only because the guy was a world champion fighter, but mostly because he was Tara's dad.

"Your lip's bleeding a little," Billy said. "I went up to have you slip a punch, but you moved a little."

That was a lie, and both of them knew it.

Trey had been tagged in the mouth.

He licked his teeth, tasting blood.

"It's not that bad," Billy said. "It's just a little blood on your bottom lip, cracked ya a little bit. It's not dripping or anything. Busted lips happen. I'd probably stay on the mat with that one, but you can stop if you want to. You can go tend to it. We can be done if you want."

"I'm okay," Trey said shaking his head a little.

And for the next thirty minutes, Billy took Trey through a grueling workout.

After it was all said and done, Billy said Trey should come back and get a membership, but in this moment, Trey wasn't so sure. He was nauseated when they finished and his lip was swollen from the inside and tasted like blood. Plus, he was a little mad. He knew Billy had tagged him for talking about Tara. He couldn't say that he blamed the man for being protective of her, but in this moment, Trey didn't feel like going to the office to sign membership papers

He went to the side to put his gloves away and get his things. He was dripping with sweat, and he felt like he'd rather go home and take a shower before he ran into Tara.

But that wasn't meant to happen. She was at the front of the gym, cleaning the guest coffee pot when he walked out. He was frustrated, and he wanted to take her and kiss her stubbornly right there in front of everyone.

"Hey," she said as he approached.

Tara's expression grew concerned the second she saw his face.

"What happened?"

"Oh, it was nothing. It was just an accident."

"With my dad?"

"Yeah, but it was my fault," he said.

"I forgot you would be here when I came in," she said. "Did you have fun?"

"I did," he said.

"How did your meeting go?" she asked.

"With your dad?" he asked.

"No. I can see how that went. I was talking about with Todd."

"Oh, fine. He's going to get the cabinets out and refinish the floors. I'm going to schedule other stuff around him."

Chapter 10

Tara

Trey seemed a little off when I saw him at the gym. He was dripping with sweat and his lip was cut. I figured my dad put him through a hard workout. He left right away, and I knew I wouldn't see him until later tonight, if I saw him at all.

We had fun with each other yesterday, but we hadn't made plans to see each other again. It bothered me that Trey left the gym so quickly after his workout. I went to my dad and asked him, point blank.

"Did you take it hard on him? Did you say something to him?"

"Who? What are you talking about?"

"Trey. Did you say something to him?"

"Of course I said something to him. He was here for a long time. I said lots of things to him."

"Did you bust his lip on purpose?"

"I wouldn't say it was on purpose. I didn't set out to make him bleed, so, no. But I did hit him."

"Dad!"

"I just popped him a little bit. It was instinct. My hand just went out, and I didn't realize how long that pad was. He took it fine."

"You're not doing me any favors if you chase him off, Dad. I have a lot depending on whether that guy likes me or not."

"What's that mean?" Dad asked, scowling.

"It means that right now the only promise I have that I'll be able to live in my apartment for another year is a handshake. Plus, I'm trying to get him to give me a deal on the downstairs."

"You don't need to do him favors to get deals on your rent," Dad said.

"I know," I said. "I'm not saying I do him favors, I'm just asking you not to punch him in the face anymore."

"He's at a boxing gym," Dad said, laughing. "And it was mostly an accident. I misjudged the pads, and he moved a little. He got his bell rung, though. I could see him blinking at me. But he recovered well. Afterwards, I put him through that workout Dizzy used to have me do."

I made a long groaning noise of disapproval at my dad, and hoped Trey wasn't mad at me for what happened.

Mondays were a long day for me.

I had to work at the gym during the afternoon, and then I taught two ballet classes on Monday evenings. I went by the apartment on my break, but I didn't see Trey.

I didn't get home until eight o'clock that evening. Trey's vehicle was out front, but I didn't see any action in the apartment when I walked by.

I was hungry, and the first thing I wanted to do was eat. I had made chicken salad earlier in the day, and I used it to fix a sandwich for myself and one for Trey. I ate mine quickly before freshening up. And then I went to take Trey the one I made for him.

I knocked on his door, but no one came. I stood in the hall for a few seconds, waiting, but he didn't seem to be there. I had the feeling he was in the secret room. I went to the place on the wall where I thought the room might be situated on the other side. I knocked on that strategic spot, and I listened, but I didn't hear Trey respond.

I decided to try to go downstairs in case he had left the door to the jewelry store open. His sandwich was on a paper plate that was covered with a napkin, and I carried it with me. It was dark out. I ran into someone on the sidewalk, but I just acted normal and said hello to them. There were no lights on in the store, but I didn't think that meant much. I went to a different window, but I still couldn't see the hallway with the secret closet. I felt like he was in there, though. I actually considered going onto the roof so that I could try to find the location of the former skylight and knock on it.

I didn't want to push myself on him, though. Having tentative plans to give him a chicken sandwich didn't seem like enough of a reason to go onto the roof and track him down.

I decided it was best to head home. I was halfway up the steps that led to my apartment when I heard the door open behind me.

"Tara," he said my name and I turned.

"Did you just try to come next door?" he asked, motioning behind him.

I nodded.

"I thought I heard you knock from upstairs a minute ago," he added. "That's why I came down.

"I did knock from upstairs," I said. "From the hallway. I wanted to see if you were hungry."

I was about five steps up on the staircase that led to our apartments, and I leaned down, handing him the plate when I saw him coming toward me like he was interested.

"I'm starving," he said, taking it from me.

He peeled back the napkin, and when he saw what it was, he used the napkin to pick up a half a sandwich. He took a bite that was so big, it would only take four of them to finish the whole sandwich. He was standing on the second and third steps and I was a step or two above him, and we just stood there, leaning against the wall and the rail while he ate.

"Thank you," he said, between bites. "I ate before I went to that tour of your dad's gym earlier, and I've been doing nothing but bustin' my hump since then. I'm starving."

"I see that you're hump-busting," I said. "You have dust in your hair." I reached out and brushed it off of him, being careful not to get it on his sandwich. "What have you been doing?"

"I got it all cleaned out, the passageway and the closet and everything. I wiped it and scrubbed and then oiled that wood. I'm not done, but I got to a lot of it. It's crazy how dusty it was. I also got the lights working upstairs, and I oiled the lever. The back wall opens faster now."

He took another bite of food, staring into space like he was contemplating something.

"I'm going to build shelves in that closet, but I'll do them facing the other way so that the trap door still works. I feel like I could make the door trigger with a book on a shelf like we were talking about."

"Oh, man, that would be magical," I said.

"It is already. It's even more amazing up there now that I have light. I can't wait until the skylight is working again. I called a contractor friend in Nashville, and he's sending a few guys to get started on it this week. I'm going to let them do the whole thing. They're good guys, and I trust them. And they live in Nashville, so they don't really care about a building in Texas with a secret passage."

"That sounds like a great idea," I said.

Trey only had a couple of bites left, and he finished it up and folded the plate.

"I'll take it upstairs to the trash," I said, reaching out for it.

He didn't hand it to me, and I looked at him inquisitively.

"I thought you were coming with me," he said. "I thought you'd want to see what all I did up there."

"I do," I said instantly. "I didn't know if you were going back over there, or if I was... " I trailed off, when he took off in the direction of the jewelry store, motioning for me to follow him. We walked out of the apartment, down the sidewalk, and into the vacant corner store. He went directly toward the back, left-hand side of the store and into the closet. I got in with him, smiling at how much cleaner everything looked.

"You did a lot of work in here," I said.

But I didn't have long to check it out because he closed the door. I was looking at him from only a foot or so away when it went dark in the closet.

He reached up and pulled the lever. He leaned into me, putting his hand on my arm to steady me and give himself a little leverage. He left his hand on my arm for a few seconds, and my heart was beating so hard I thought he could maybe feel it pounding just from touching my arm.

He let me go as the door opened.

This happened far too quickly.

"It works a lot better now," he said, smiling at me and letting go. "See how fast it opens?"

"I know! How?" I asked, trying not to sound disappointed.

"I pulled back some more of the wall and oiled the mechanism."

"Oh, wow, it's a lot lighter in here today," I said when the back wall opened, revealing the stairway. The stairway and the wood paneling were both more visible today, and it was beautiful.

Trey was no longer touching my arm, and I was able to concentrate on other things. "Oh, Trey, this is so gorgeous." I breathed in as I came to stand at the base of the stairs. "Did you clean these walls?"

Everything looked shiny. The walls were made of beautiful slats of wood running floor-to-ceiling, and I touched them as I began to walk up the spiral staircase.

"I wiped them and then put this protective wood conditioner on them. Your uncle sold it to me."

I knew he had cleaned. It smelled good—the light scent of pine and citrus. He climbed the stairs, and I followed him. "I cannot believe you did all this in one day," I said, marveling at how different it was.

"I know. I did a lot this morning, but then I went at it this afternoon. I had to blow off some steam."

"If that's about my dad, I'm sorry. He did like you. He told me you were good."

"It's fine," he said. "I might have done the same thing in his position. I just needed a minute to cool-down and recover from that workout. I came over here and worked, and compared to that workout, it was like a vacation."

I laughed at him. I was really relieved that he wasn't mad.

"Besides, I had to clean it. I had to see what was going on in here. It's going to get dirty again once construction starts, but I wanted to see what I was working with. One thing led to another, and I just ended up working like mad."

"It looks unbelievable," I said, marveling at how shiny it was with the lights on. There were two of them... wall sconces that lit up the room with a soft amber glow. "I can't believe you got all this done so fast." I gazed at the shelves, which were polished and glossy.

"I've done nothing but work this afternoon. I didn't even realize what time it was. I had music playing. I almost didn't hear you knock. I'm surprised I did. It's just because I was right there by that wall."

I stood in the middle of the room. It was beautiful, and I was stuck in there with my prince charming. I felt like I was in a dream. I turned and made eye contact with Trey. He still had the radio on, but he had turned it down. "This is wonderful," I said. "It's just really... perfect."

I took the next couple of minutes to check it out and take it all in. The lights and cleaning made a gigantic difference.

Trey had a big paper cup from a gas station. He took a sip of whatever was in it, and I asked him if I could have one as well. He warned me that the ice was mostly melted and then he grinned at me for being willing to drink out of his cup. We shared a few seconds of eye contact, and my heart sped up, but we didn't say anything. I took a sip. It was iced tea, and it tasted great.

"Wait till I get that window working," he said, changing the subject as I set the cup down. "And I'm having thoughts about a different exit route." He pointed to the spiral staircase that led downstairs. "I'm thinking about extending the stairs and making a better exit to the roof from this room. Because, even with the ladder and a window that opens, this would be an emergency exit only. I can't imagine going in and out of a window."

I pictured stairs leading to the roof. They would only take up a little corner of the room, and it would be neat to have an official exit route.

"I think that would be amazing," I said. "Plus, the spiral stairs look so cool that they would be pretty in this room. Do you think you could get some that look similar? Where do you even get spiral stairs?"

"I'm having that contractor look at everything. He'll be here later this week. If all else fails, I could just have a staircase custom made, though. For the right price, you can have anything made."

I walked over to the wall on my right, leaning against it and trying to imagine the stairs going up to the ceiling. They would be really cool in this room.

"Is this 202?" I asked, touching the wall behind me.

"Yes. I brought a compass up here to make sure. But yeah, that's the storage closet, and the one you're touching is 202."

I turned and leaned against the wall to his apartment. "It would be really cool to put a door right here. You know, sometime, eventually, I might rent that space downstairs, and if you were ever in town visiting and you stayed in 202, you could use this passage to... come get me if you need anything."

"Oh, while you're downstairs in your ballet studio?"

"Yeah, well, what did you decide with 202? Are you renting it to someone else, or are you going to keep it vacant and stay there when you visit Galveston? Because if it's basically your apartment, it'd be cool for you to have access to this room."

He stepped closer to me, and I felt my heart speed up. "What's an ideal scenario for you, Tara?" He stood right beside me, and I stared at his face, at his mouth. My heart was beating faster and faster the closer he got.

"Your lip," I said regretfully when my eye fell onto his cut.

"It's nothing."

"I'm sorry," I said. "And my dad was sorry, too."

The corners of his mouth rose in a wry smile. "Was he?" Trey asked.

Chapter 11

"Yes, he was sorry," I said. "He said he did it by accident."

"Okay," Trey conceded, nodding. But I could tell he didn't quite believe me.

"Did it bust on the inside?" I asked, still inspecting his lip. There was a little bulge near the cut, but it looked good on him—it made him look tough. Staring at his mouth, inspecting his cut, proved to me one thing... that I desperately wanted to kiss Trey Harper. My stomach tied into a big pile of knots as my eyes roamed over his mouth. Goodness gracious, I was breathless.

"What do you mean did it bust on the inside?" he asked. He was smiling at me when he asked the question, and I watched his mouth, the way it moved when he spoke and when he smiled.

Oh, no. This was bad. I wasn't sure if I had ever wanted to kiss someone as badly as I wanted to kiss Trey right then. It was with great difficulty that I stopped myself from doing it. I had to do something to get my mind off of pressing my lips to his. I reached up carefully, placing my palm against his jaw. I used my thumb to gently prod the area near his cut in a detached, professional way, like a doctor would.

"I was wondering if you had a big, busted lip on the inside, or if it's just cut from the outside," I said.

I made a face like it was all very clinical and I was concentrating as I felt the area near his mouth. Then the butterflies took over, and I quickly let him go.

"It's doesn't feel like it's that bad," I said.

"It's not," he said.

"But I'm still sorry."

"It's all right. I can't say that I blame him."

"Why?"

"Because he's protective. I told him I like you."

"Did he do it on purpose?" I asked with a serious expression.

"Yes. But it's not that big of a deal. He doesn't know me. He doesn't know what my intentions are. For all he knows, I could be making you feel like you owe me something because of the deal with the rent."

"But you aren't," I said.

"Yeah, but your dad doesn't know that. Plus, he's Billy Castro. I sort of feel like I'm getting off easy with a little busted lip."

He smiled, and I dropped my hand and smiled back at him.

"I didn't mean for you to stop," he said.

"Stop what?" I asked.

"The check-up. The stuff you were looking at on my face."

My grin broadened when I understood what he was saying. I moved a little closer as a distraction to myself.

108

"It's not too bad," I said, feeling too shy to reach up and touch his lip again.

"What? You barely even looked at it," he said.

"I did look at it," I said. My eyes roamed over his jaw, neck, shirt, chest, and then neck again. He was being patient, being quiet, waiting for me to look at him. I let my eyes meet his, and his mouth moved just enough that I caught the hint of a smile.

"In a fantasy world, I own my own ballet studio in this beautiful building. I'd have this whole hallway off limits to students, and I'd disappear back into this closet and climb a staircase wall where I'd find a secret room. I'd get to come up here and kiss a handsome prince, and then I'd go back downstairs where I'd finish teaching ballet."

"Am I a handsome prince in this story?" he asked. "Because I couldn't quite tell."

"Yea-absolutely," I said.

"Because I didn't set out to trap a ballerina when I took over this building. This happened by accident." He spoke slowly and thoughtfully, his deep voice sounding soft and low like velvet. I was breathless. I looked around slowly and then back at Trey.

"If this is a trap, then I've thought of traps all wrong. I thought it was only a trap if the one who's caught doesn't want to be there."

Trey started leaning closer, looking at me, putting his face closer to mine. My heart was beating like a wild bird. I looked up and he ducked, putting his mouth right next to my cheek. I could feel him against my skin.

"You are beautiful," he said.

I reached out and placed my hand on his arm. We were close to the wall, but I was dizzy with adrenaline and anticipation, so it felt good to have him there to steady me.

"I could see myself building a door right here if I thought you'd appear on the other side of it," he said.

"If you build a door there, you should never rent it out again. It would just have to be your place."

"I might try to come to Galveston more frequently if I thought you wanted me to."

I stared up at him, feeling like he was taller than six-two.

"I thought you assumed I wanted you to come by now," I said. "And if you do come back, you have to promise to go back to the gym," I said. "I don't want you to worry about the busted lip."

"I'm not worried about it," he said.

"Good, then, neither of us are worried," I said.

"Good," he said.

"But, seriously, you should put doors and windows where you want," I added. "Don't listen to me when I'm talking about making a—"

I stopped talking in mid-sentence because Trey leaned down and kissed me. He let his mouth touch mine, and I held on for dear life as an overwhelming wave of joy and relief washed over me. It felt so good. My body was cool and electric. We had been close to this the night before, and all of today, I had looked forward to this moment. I leaned into it, and Trey adjusted, licking his lips and kissing me again.

One, two, three gentle, warm, slick kisses.

His mouth was soft but not too soft. It felt perfect. It felt like I knew it would feel. Trey was an experienced kisser. He never made a wrong move.

I was in love.

***

Trey kissed me several other times during the days that followed. We had seen each other quite a bit. He had a productive week of contracting work and negotiating the other property, and he would leave for Nashville, as planned, in the morning.

Trey and I definitely had chemistry. There was no doubt that we were attracted to each other. But at the same time, we had plenty of time spent talking or cleaning—doing things where we weren't getting close to each other.

I helped him continue to clean the secret room. It was so much better on the first day, that I didn't realize how much still needed to be done. I worked Wednesday morning and Thursday afternoon, helping him get all the crevices and high places.

On his last day, Trey went to another boxing session, and my father had worn him out again. He sparred with Trey, taking him to his limits. Trey was athletic enough, but it was impossible for him to keep up with my father who was a master at his craft.

Dad put him through the wringer for two hours. I watched it happen, feeling like I was witnessing some sort of rite of passage. I didn't apologize to Trey for the fact that it happened, but I did let him know I was proud of him for enduring it. He said that he could tell my dad had good intentions. He seemed to understand that my dad's actions stemmed from a place of love and protection. I was just happy that he wasn't frustrated. He was physically spent afterwards, though, and we had to pause for some food and a break, but he was still in a good mood.

We spent time in the secret room that evening, listening to music while we worked. Several times, Trey busted out singing or dancing. He didn't normally speak with a heavy southern drawl, but he imitated country music, and I marveled at how spot on he was. I didn't usually like country music, but something about hearing it come out of the mouth of a handsome man really added to the appeal. He did it as a joke, but I secretly liked it.

Trey and I laughed and goofed off together. It was like we had always known each other. And just like that, it was Thursday night, and we were saying goodbye.

I had no idea when I would see him again. His next trip to Galveston was scheduled for next month when he signed papers on the pink building.

It could be a month before I saw him again.

Things were likely to work out that way.

We had already talked about me keeping an eye on the renovations. Trey told Todd and his contractor from Nashville about me and told them that I would be his go-between.

We had talked a lot about the building renovations. He decided to put a door leading into the secret room from apartment 202. Because of the compact area they were working with, it would be more of a half door, and it would be, again, disguised as a bookshelf. Trey hired teams of quality craftsmen to build specialty pieces, and a select crew from Nashville do the demolition, construction, and installation. I couldn't wait to see the results.

Trey and I had been in the room all evening, and then just like that, we decided to leave. It was time to say goodnight. We reluctantly left the secret room. He turned and waited for me when we got to the closet at the bottom of the steps. We had turned out the light upstairs, so the distant nightlight was all the light we had. It was near dark.

Trey reached out for me, touching my arm. "I have two things to talk to you about, and I can't believe I waited until now. I don't know if I'll see you in the morning. I don't think I will, and I need to tell you these two things. I'm sorry I'm just now thinking of this. We can do it here or go upstairs to one of the apartments, if you want."

"Now I'm so curious I want you to just say it right here."

"One is that I wanted you to know I'm going to rent the downstairs to you. I figured we hinted at it before, but I wanted to say officially that I am planning on letting you move in downstairs. I decided that. I'm in the process of writing up the lease, but I won't go up much, if any at all, from what Mister McCain was paying."

I tightened up instinctually, my toes curling with excitement. I wanted to squeal, and I had to hold myself back. "Thank you," I said.

"And I really don't want you to feel like you owe me anything," he said. "I'm happy to have you here. I know you'll take care of the place, and eventually, when your dance school is busting at the seams, you can pay me what the building's worth."

I hugged him tightly.

"I am so excited, you have no idea."

He held me back. My eyes had adjusted to the darkness of the closet, and I stared at the paneling on the back wall, taking a mental snapshot of the way I felt in this moment, in this dark, cramped room. It was a tangible feeling of bliss.

"What's the second thing?" I asked.

"Oh, that… uh… this one's… maybe I should have given you that first one last because it was the good news."

"Is the next one something bad?" I asked.

"No, no, it's not bad, it's just a little… I don't know, awkward, maybe. Honestly, I don't think it

114

happening is awkward I just sort of feel awkward about telling you about it."

"Oh, now I'm dying to know," I said, pulling back and trying to focus on him in the dark closet.

"No, now I've built it up too much. I'm sure you're not even going to care. It's just a wedding. I'm going to a wedding in Mexico. I don't even know the people. My friend, Beth, she's the maid of honor at this wedding, and everybody's taking dates so she asked me to go down there with her so she won't be alone. It's not that we're dating, we're not, but she had asked me to this wedding with her a few months ago, and we're old friends, so I said I would. I had this planned, not knowing that I would be spending time with you, and it's—"

"It's totally fine," I said. I was so elated with the news about the building that, in that moment, I would do or say anything to keep him from changing his mind about it.

"It is?" he said. "You don't care?"

"No, no, no, I'm not, we're not, I mean, I know you had plans ahead of time, and you and I hadn't even talked about things like that."

"So, it doesn't bother you at all?"

"No, no, honestly, not at all. I'm glad that's all it was. I got scared for a second when you said it was bad news."

"Okay. Are you sure?"

"Yeah, definitely. When even is it?"

"In three weeks," he said. "I'll go home to Nashville afterward, but then I'll turn around and come here."

"Yeah, you definitely shouldn't pass up a trip to Mexico," I said. "Don't factor me into that kind of thing. I really don't care."

Chapter 12

A month later

I cared, I cared, I cared so much.

I told Trey that I did not care if he went to Mexico on an extended, glamourous wedding vacation as a date to a most-likely-beautiful woman, but I cared. I cared way more than I thought I would.

Dang it.

I had no idea why I was so nonchalant when he talked to me about that blasted trip to Mexico. I basically begged him to go. *What had I been thinking?* I experienced regret and jealousy in full force during the month that followed. I had to make a conscious choice to not obsess about the regret.

I talked to Trey during the three weeks before his trip, but I didn't let all of my walls down. We talked about neutral topics, like construction and general progress on the building. It was difficult to keep my distance when I was so tempted to give in to the fairytale feeling of it all, but I just couldn't let myself be vulnerable with that trip coming up.

Todd completed his work on the downstairs in no time. He was aware that there was construction on the roof, but I told him it was happening upstairs, which was the truth and all he needed to know. I had fun managing things, and I found myself downstairs quite a bit, making plans and watching progress. I talked to Trey, but I mostly kept it work related. In the back of my mind, he would go to the wedding and things would happen that would result in getting my heart broken. I felt like I was holding my breath until he got that trip over with.

And finally, after what seemed like a year, ten years even, it was time for Trey to come back to Galveston.

So much had happened with the building that I couldn't believe it had only been a month since his last visit. The secret room was totally transformed. Apartment 202 also had work done, and I was extremely excited for Trey to see all of it.

It was Friday afternoon when he arrived in Galveston. I had been in close enough contact with him that I knew he would be there by dinner time.

I was nervous, and things had been slightly distant between us, but I wanted to give him a warm welcome, so I cooked a meal. I pulled out all the stops, making three dishes even though I was normally used to cooking quick and easy things by myself. I cooked homemade macaroni and cheese, some steak, which I had already sliced, and green beans.

I was sweaty from all the scrambling in the kitchen, and I decided to take a quick shower before he arrived. I left it to stay warm on the stove while I freshened up. I rushed to get it all done, but he took longer to get there than I anticipated.

I was just about to walk over to his apartment when my phone rang.

"Hello?" I said, answering the phone on the first ring.

"Hey," Trey said.

"Hey, did you make it?"

"Yeah, I'm in Galveston. But I'm stuck at the airport. Not for good. But for an hour or so. The rental had a flat, and it was all they had, so they're changing it."

"I'll pick you up," I said, instantly.

"Oh, no don't worry about it. I'll need the truck anyway. And it's already been a while since they told me it would be an hour. It's probably more like thirty minutes now. It'll go fast. I just thought I'd check in with you since I told you my flight landed at five."

"I'm glad you did," I said. "I made dinner. I was about to put it in the fridge."

"You made dinner?" I could tell he was smiling when he asked the question. His voice got softer and it sounded like he got closer to the phone.

It was the first time in a month that I let myself respond to any flirtatiousness, and the feeling was electrifying.

"Yes, I made dinner, and I felt like a chef in here with four pots going at once. I don't know what I was thinking. I already had to take… never mind. Where are you? I want you to come over."

"I'm at the airport, on a payphone," he said.

"And thank you for cooking. I'm looking forward to eating some of whatever you made."

"Steak and mac-n-cheese."

"I can't wait."

"Do you need me to let you go since you're on a payphone?"

"No," he said. "Nobody's around."

I smiled as I carried my cordless phone across the room to sit on the couch.

"I'm relieved you're in Galveston," I said.

"Are you?"

"Why would you ask it like that?" I asked.

"Because I'm surprised. You've been all business for the last month."

"No, I haven't," I insisted. But I knew he was right, so I corrected myself. "It's only because I was scared of Mexico, a little."

"Why were you scared? You told me you weren't scared."

"I told you that," I said. "And I didn't mean to lie, but I guess I was scared. I had a whole thing built-up in my mind. I thought maybe you'd get married while you were over there, like you might come back with a new wife or something."

He laughed at that. "A *new wife*?" he said in a disbelieving tone that made me feel happy.

"I don't know. I thought, I was scared, since we didn't talk about things and I acted like I didn't care, I thought you might, I don't know, it sounds funny to say it now, but I thought you were going to come back married."

"Yeah, I didn't do that."

"Somebody tried to, but I told them I couldn't."

"What? Who? What are you saying? Somebody tried to marry you? Beth?"

"Yes," he said, smiling at my apparent impatience. "It was Beth. But no, she didn't quite try to marry me."

"What happened?"

"Nothing," he said. "She tried to kiss me, but I didn't let it happen.

I concentrated on containing my emotion. "Really? Did she try?"

"Do you care?" he asked.

"Yes," I said.

"You said you didn't before."

"Well, I was wrong for saying that. Did you do it? Did you kiss her?"

"No."

"You didn't?"

"No, I didn't. We had a whole argument. She asked why I wasn't letting it happen, and I told her I was talking to someone."

I knew that someone was me, and I was inexplicably excited. "So, nothing happened?"

"No. Nothing at all."

"Was it because of this other woman you're talking to?" I asked.

"Yes."

"Who is she?" I asked.

"You know who. You better know who."

"I know. I think I know," I said.

"If you don't know, I'm going to be really disappointed when I see you in a little while."

Bump-bump, bump-bump, bump-bump.

My heart was steadily beating.

"You're not going to believe this apartment," I said, trying to change the subject before I did something crazy like start crying from happiness. "And the stairs and everything. It's all so beautiful. I think you're going to be really happy with it."

"I want you to give me the grand tour."

"I can't wait to," I said. "Come to my apartment first, and we'll walk over there together."

"Okay, I will. I'm relieved that you want to see me," he said. "I thought maybe your dad forbid you to see me."

"Forbid me? No. Dad had nothing to do with it. I was just seeing how Mexico played out."

"It played out that I thought you barely liked me, Tara, and I still wouldn't talk to anyone else."

I smiled even though he couldn't see me. "I'm happy you're here. You're not going to believe the room."

"Do you love it?"

"It's more than I ever dreamed. That back wall closes now when you're upstairs. There's a little switch. It's amazing. Totally hidden. It looks like a little closet. It *is* a closet. It's functional, and

122

everything's so hidden. It's perfect. You're going to love it. Did that girl really try to kiss you?"

He chuckled. "Yes. It was a whole thing. She cried."

"She cried? Seriously?"

"Yes."

"Why didn't you tell me?"

"Because I wasn't sure if you cared. I was going to see you in person and get a feel."

"I care," I said. "I'm not happy that she cried, but I'm happy about what it implies."

"What, exactly, does it imply?" he asked.

"That you like me."

"I think I do," he said.

"Good," I returned. "Are you sure you don't want me to go pick you up at the airport?"

"No, thank you, I'll be there in a few minutes."

We hung up the phone, and Trey pulled up on Bank Street thirty minutes later.

I was positioned where I could see outside, so I noticed the movement of cars and I glanced out all the time. I had an extra hour to prepare for his arrival, and I still felt like I had to rush around at the last minute. I was cleaning some dust near the window when he pulled up and parked. It was a beautiful early summer day, and I had the window open.

"Hey there," I called, but I was breathless and it came out quieter than I imagined. He didn't hear me.

He glanced at the window just before he went under the awning, but he didn't catch a glimpse of me.

I did some frantic, last-second straightening as I waited for him to come up the steps. I thought about standing there, in my apartment, and waiting for him, but I couldn't make myself do it.

I opened the door and looked at the stairwell, seeing the top of the back of Trey's head through the railing as he came up the stairs. I watched him walk, feeling nervous and excited. He smiled at me when he turned and came around the corner. He was dressed nicely in a button-down shirt with jeans, and he had a suitcase and a duffel bag. His facial hair had grown a little, and I smiled at how different he seemed after a month. I was done for.

"I'm going to leave this stuff in my apartment," he said. He stopped in his doorway and set down his luggage, and I just couldn't deal with it any longer. I went over to him because I couldn't wait. I thought about that woman trying to kiss him and wondered if he would kiss me. I was drawn to him, and I wanted to kiss him so badly. I wanted to make sure he would kiss me back.

He saw that I was coming, and he stopped what he was doing and smiled, holding his arms out so that I could walk into them. Trey welcomed me into his arms, taking me into an instant embrace. I thought we might break apart after a couple of seconds, but we didn't. We just stood there and held each other in the hallway. Twice, I almost said something, but I changed my mind. I just held him and let him hold me.

"Hello, Tara," he said eventually. It had been at least a full minute, maybe two.

I leaned back so that I could focus on his face. I smiled, and it caused him to smile back.

"Hi," I said.

"Hi."

"I was thinking about you."

His grin broadened. "Oh yeah? What were you thinking?"

"All sorts of stuff. I'm happy about Mexico. And I'm happy you're in Texas."

Just then, Charlotte and Mickey came into the downstairs apartment door. They were at the bottom of the steps where they couldn't see us, and we had plenty of time to separate and not get caught embracing. It was so frustrating that they came in right when we saw each other for the first time in a month.

"Just go," Trey whispered, looking at me with an urgent expression.

I turned and took off with no hesitation. Trey picked up his luggage, and we took off, as fast as we could, to my place, running and moving out of the way just in time for me to open the door.

I stood back and let him run through.

It was comical how close they were to seeing us.

I closed the door just in time for them to make it to the top of the stairway and look back at me. I had been watching the backs of their heads. I waved at them, as I closed the door.

They had no idea that Trey had just run into my apartment, and the close call had me laughing after I closed the door. Trey had gone into my kitchen so that he was out of view, and I instantly went in there to meet him. He had already put down his bags and I went his way, both of us laughing as I landed right next to him.

"We would have been stuck talking for twenty minutes," he said.

"I know. We did good."

"They can't see us now," he said. He smiled irresistibly and placed his hand on the back of my waist, pulling me closer. I stretched up and kissed his cheek, breaking the ice since I didn't know how else to start. I leaned over and kissed his other cheek after that, and then I kissed his mouth. He kissed me back, and our mouths met in a gentle perfect soft peck. It was the most perfect little kiss that had ever happened. I felt a zap of electricity when our mouths met.

I pulled back, smiling at Trey. He stared at me, his brown eyes searching my face. There was no telling what he would say next. I was quiet, regarding him and waiting. My hands were on his arms, and I let my fingertips roam over the ridges of muscles along his triceps.

"You are terrible at long distance relationships," he said, staring at me. "I had no clue I would get this kind of reception. I didn't even know you still liked me."

I smiled and leaned up to kiss him again. For a second time, we executed a perfect, barely-open-mouthed kiss.

"I'm sorry," I whispered afterward. "I was so scared about Mexico."

"You should have told me that, Tara. Beth Hardwick has nothing on you."

Just hearing her name caused me to experience a stab of jealousy.

"I don't know what to say other than I'm so happy you didn't do anything with her."

"I didn't. I was thinking about you."

"Thank you. I don't want you to kiss anyone else, please." I had kissed Trey twice and he had let me do it both times. He had kissed me back. He did not kiss Beth, and he did kiss me. I was the one he had chosen. I felt all melty inside, and I clung to him, burying my face in his chest and holding and hugging him for another few seconds before letting him go.

"Do you want to eat first, or go see the room?" I asked.

"I don't really feel like leaving your apartment right this second," he said. "You can catch me up on things while we eat, and then you can take me to see it in a minute."

Chapter 13

He ate, and we talked for about an hour while we sat in my kitchen.

His smile. Goodness. It was mesmerizing. His eyes squinted, and his teeth flashed in a way that left me breathless every time. I was enamored even more now than I had been a month ago.

I was glad I thought ahead. I had a whole thing planned out for when I revealed the new and improved secret room, and it was difficult for me to contain my excitement about it. Trey knew I was excited to show him the renovations, but he didn't know the extent of my surprise. I acted laidback about it, letting him eat and talking to him for a while before I even mentioned going to look at the progress in the room. I followed him to apartment 202.

He thought we would go through the new passageway together, but I stopped him before we even got close to the new trapdoor.

"You know how the handle works, and the door," I said. "I'm going to let you do it."

"Are you not going in with me?" he asked. He looked disappointed, and it made me happy.

"I am, I'm just, I'm going the other way."

"Well, I'll go the other way with you," he said.

"I'm going alone, and you're going through here," I said, staring at him, letting him know that I had something brewing.

"There's a chair in the corner, and you'll find a note."

"Are you good?" he asked, looking slightly concerned.

"Yes. It's all good. I'm just excited to show it to you. I'm doing something. I'm going in the other way. Give me a second to get down there. Wait right here for two minutes, and then go in and find the note. It's in a chair in the corner." I was retreating to the other side of the room as I spoke. We were both smiling—him at me for being nervous and in a hurry, and me because I was so excited. "I'll see you in a minute," I added.

I left his apartment and instantly ran down the staircase and out the door that led to the sidewalk. I had thought about this moment for weeks and rehearsed it in my mind so much that I knew exactly what I was going to do.

I ran into Papaw King who owned the hardware store next door, and I said 'hey Papaw' so fast that he laughed at me.

I moved swiftly, hugging corners, and slipping into the door of my new studio. Trey had gotten a coating put on the windows. It was a subtle mirror finish. You could see out from the inside but not the other way around. I had total privacy as soon as I closed the door.

I locked it behind me and took off toward the hall bathroom.

I had everything set up. I stripped down to my ballet costume. It wasn't a full costume. It was basically a fancier version of the leotards that I wear all the time. I was wearing a black, short-sleeve leotard with a detailed scoop neck. I also had on a sheer black skirt. I wore nude tights and leather slippers, and I tied my hair into a neat bun.

I was nice and tight looking, like a proper ballerina. But the black leotard was my favorite—it went with my hair.

I knew what I had to do. I had practiced this enough, and I had been in the downstairs so much in the last month that this process was quick and easy.

I changed and tied up my hair, and just like that, I was heading for the closet. I stepped inside of it, closed the door, and pulled the lever (which was now attached to a fake book). The trap door opened quietly, and I stepped out of the closet and into the secret room. I pushed a button to close the door behind me, and I stood at the foot of the steps, feeling more nervous than I had ever been in my entire life.

I had to assume that Trey was already in the secret room, waiting for me. "Are you there?" I said, calling up the steps and hoping he could hear me.

"Yes." I heard his deep voice answer me, and I thought I might melt into a pool of mushy goo right there.

"Did you read your note?" I asked.

"I did," he said. "I'm sitting where you told me to sit."

"Isn't it beautiful up there?"

"It is..." He hesitated, and a few seconds of silence passed before he added, "But I want you up here with me."

"I'm coming," I promised, feeling nervous and doubting myself more and more with every passing second. I gave myself a mental pep talk as I pressed the button on my boombox to start the music.

I had the volume adjusted and I strategically positioned the device where the speaker projected up the stairs. I recorded a tape for my dance. The music started softly with a slow intro that led into a three-minute piece called the Carnival of the Animals, and then it would go into beautiful, slow classical music for thirty minutes before fading away. My dance was only three minutes, but I wanted music to continue afterward.

I was shaken, but I trusted myself, knowing that at one point I thought this was all a good idea. I heard the music begin, and I started climbing the steps. I was in character immediately. I was a fairy, trapped in a jar. The song began, and I did my dance. It was a ballet that was made for Trey. I told a whole story through movement.

I could see Trey out of the corner of my eye as I danced. I choreographed the piece for the room, tailoring it for the person who would be sitting in the

131

chair. I could see him watching me, but I couldn't let myself look straight at him because if I did, I might break character. I made a conscious choice to devote myself to the dance. I was aware of Trey sitting there, but I didn't let myself look at him or be affected by him.

I was so full of adrenaline that I performed the whole thing feeling a bit like I was outside of my own body. In the story, I spent the majority of the time climbing and flying and twisting and turning, trying my best to get out of the room before finally coming to the realization that I was staying there, at which time I collapsed blissfully onto the floor.

The music got quieter and I stayed still, feeling winded and spent and doing my best to regulate my breathing. I stayed there for several long heartbeats, on my back, staring at the ceiling while the music continued to play. I was relieved and tired, and the music and feelings seemed to swirl all around me. I saw it out of my periphery when Trey got out of the chair and came over to me. He sat down beside me leaning over me curiously.

"Tara?" he said, whispering my name.

"Yeah?" I said, whispering back.

"That was un-be-lieve-able. What was that just now?"

"A dance," I said, still catching my breath. I knew he loved it by the way he was acting, and it made me so happy. I could feel and see my own chest rising and falling as I breathed.

Trey sat next to me and he leaned over, checking me out, looking me over. "Did you make that up just now?" he asked.

I let out a humorless laugh, thinking about all the hours upon hours of work it took to make that look the way it did. "Nooo," I said, chuckling a little. "That was planned."

He leaned closer to me, hovering over me. My eyes met his. The big lights were on dimmers, and I had them turned down for the performance. I also hung string lights that my dad had in the garage from Christmas. It was a magical room, and I had taken time to make it extra special for him.

"We don't have to leave the lights up," I said. "I just put them up for the welcome party."

"The lights are great," he said. "But I still haven't finished talking about that dance you just did."

I was lying flat on my back, and I wiggled a little, getting closer to him. I tucked my legs and turned to the side, still lying down but making a posture like I was clinging onto him even though we weren't touching.

"I was dancing for you," I said. "To welcome you to your new room."

"I couldn't care less about this room right now," he said dazedly.

"Trey!" I said, getting onto him even though I loved what he was saying.

"I'm just kiddin', I love the room." He paused and stared upward, checking out the stairs and the new window. "This place is a masterpiece."

I still worked to steady my breathing, but it was getting easier now that I was relaxing. He leaned over me, staring at me like he wanted to do something crazy. I grinned and squirmed. The music played softly and the late afternoon light spilled through the skylight and shone behind him. He was like an angel in that light. It was a moment I would always remember. If I were a painter like my mother, I would certainly paint this scene.

"You did a lot of work in here," he said, speaking softly. "Not just on that dance, but also on this room. What's that chair all about? I was checking everything out before you came in. You got that chair, the lights, you put my books on the shelf, and that new stuff—the globe is new. So many things."

"I had the globe in a closet at my parents' house. I thought it looked good in here."

"It does," he said. "So does the chair."

"I knew you'd like the chair. It's the one you talked about last time you were here."

"I know," he said. "How did it get here?"

"I bought it. I wanted to set the room up a little bit for when you saw it. I figured if you didn't like it in here, or you didn't want it, I could always take it back down to my apartment."

Trey turned and checked out the chair. I watched him as he looked at it. He was quiet, and I just laid there and took in the curves of the underside of his chin and jaw. I was still breathing a little heavier than usual, but I was calm compared to a minute ago. I sat up long enough to take my hair down, shaking it out and letting it fall on my shoulders. I set the clip on the floor near me and relaxed again.

I smiled up at Trey, who was just sitting there, patiently watching me. "I was calling it Dance of the Fairy in my head, but my outfit doesn't really look like a fairy. I'm missing my wings."

"I watched you thinking you're so beautiful and yet I just had the urge to reach out and capture you—to hold you still. You were so beautiful that I almost felt like I couldn't watch it."

"Did you watch?" I asked, glancing at him.

"Every single second," he said.

"Did you like it?"

"I want you to be mine, Tara Castro. Nobody's but mine. Would you please do that? Can we make that happen?"

"Yes," I said.

"Yes?"

I shrugged. "I don't just go around making dances up for guys I don't like."

"You like me?" He hovered over me, close to me, resting one hand on the other side of me for leverage. I reached up and touched him. I barely touched the back of his arm with my fingertips. "What if I do like you?" I asked, flirting with him.

"If you do, it'll be good. I'll be happy."

"I do then," I said.

He stared at me. "Can you do that again?" he asked.

"Can I do what?" I asked.

"The dance."

I let out a little laugh.

"Maybe in a few days or a week," I said. "I have to give you the chance to forget what you saw so it'll seem special again."

"I don't want to forget it. And it already is special."

I smiled and curled into him. "Just wait a day or two so you're impressed when you see it again."

He reached out and touched me. He rubbed the back of his finger down my cheek. "You were a fairy," he said.

I smiled at him as my eyes snapped to meet his. "Really? You think?"

He nodded. "You wrote that in your note, but I think I would have realized what you were doing even if you hadn't told me."

"Thank you," I said.

"Thank *you*," he returned. "I mean it, Tara. I've never seen anything like this before. I'm not even able to concentrate on the construction that happened. I don't even care. I don't want this building if you're not in it."

"I am in it," I said, reaching out and holding onto his arm. I ran my fingertips along the back side of it, touching him gently.

"Then I want it."

I stared at him. "I'm so glad you're here," I said.

Chapter 14

Trey

It was Saturday morning, and he woke up thinking about that oversized chair in the corner of the secret room. He had been thinking about Tara since their reunion last night, and this morning, his thoughts led to the chair.

Last night, she had surprised him with the room and the private ballet. Obviously, the dance itself was an amazing gift. All last evening, he was stunned by it and obsessed with locking it into his memory. He asked her more than a few times to perform it again, but she didn't.

But this morning, he woke up feeling touched at the thought of that chair. Tara's parents had done well with their chosen occupations, and they helped her out with a few of her living expenses, but they certainly didn't provide her with a lavish lifestyle. She worked and made a paycheck like a normal person, and Trey felt touched that she would buy that chair.

He wanted to give her his credit card and let her buy more things to put in that room. He wanted her to finish decorating it. She mentioned a rug, and he thought that should be the first thing they buy.

Trey could not get Tara Castro out of his mind. That dance. He wished he had recorded it. He had vivid memories of it, but he knew there were things he missed or that he was forgetting. He remembered her dancing on the staircase, climbing that new section of stairs and performing a part of the dance up there.

The two of them hung out until 2am, looking at all of the new trap door mechanisms and general construction. They went onto the roof for a while, and then at one point in the evening, they explored the downstairs where Tara would soon open a studio and gallery.

She led him through a waltz in the main studio room. The floors were beautiful, and the color she chose for the walls looked serene, soft, and peaceful. She led Trey around the whole room twice before he got the hang of it and he started leading her.

Even at two o'clock in the morning, their parting had been reluctant. Tara had plans to go to the gym at 9am, and Trey agreed to meet her there so that he could participate in the morning class.

He was tired when his alarm went off, but he woke up thinking about her, and that made it much easier to get out of bed.

Class, however, did not work out as planned.

Billy Castro coached it, and he did not take it easy on Trey. He pushed his limits at everything. He not only tested him physically, but he made quick conversation with him, testing him mentally as well.

It would have been bearable if Trey didn't have to worry about Tara the whole time.

Tara's brother, Will, was there, but Billy still made Tara partner with a young fighter named Miguel. Trey got partnered with an older guy named Quentin who used to be a fighter but now worked a regular job and went there to train on weekends. He was tough, and he took Billy's lead and didn't take it easy on Trey.

Trey tried to do the class to the best of his abilities, but he was not a trained boxer, and Billy was in the mood to test him. Eighty percent of the people at the gym were men, and a hundred percent of those men were protective of Tara. They knew Trey liked Tara, and in a way, it made him the enemy. None of them took it easy on him. They weren't mean, but at the same time, they weren't going out of their way to make him comfortable.

Trey tried not to feel frustrated about it.

He had changed and was heading out of the locker room when he overheard someone say his name from outside. He stopped short of leaving the locker room and tuned in to the conversation.

"...standing here, waiting for Trey," was the first thing he heard. It was Tara speaking, and Trey slowed down and listened. "I'm glad I saw you," she continued. "I wanted to talk to you, anyway."

"Oh really, what about?" It was Billy who answered. Tara was talking to her dad. Trey knew their voices.

"I wanted to ask you to be nicer to Trey."

"Trey's a man," Billy said. "And he's tough. I was just talking to Quentin about him. He's got some heavy hands, and some good instincts."

"I know, but Dad, I'm not talking about his boxing. I'm talking about running him off in general."

"I'm not running him off," Billy said.

"But you're not making him comfortable, either."

"I've never been comfortable a day of my life in here, training, Tara. That's the whole point of being in here, to get tough."

"You know what I mean," she said. "I'm not talking about boxing. I'm willing to let y'all sort the boxing stuff out. I just wanted to make sure you knew he was with me and that it matters to me that he likes you."

"What are you asking me, exactly?" Billy asked.

"I'm just saying that it would mean a lot to me if you make him feel like he's welcome around here. I want you to be aware of the fact that he's here with me and he's not just some other boxing student."

"Your mother was right," Billy said.

"What do you mean?"

"She told me you would intercede."

There were a few seconds of silence, after which time Tara said, "I don't get it. Are you doing this just to see how I react?"

"No," Billy said "But I do think it's interesting that you're reacting the way you are."

"Why? Did you think I would never like a guy?"

"No, you've liked plenty of guys. Twice, you've dated guys for months and just never brought them around. And the ones you did bring around, you did the whole, this-is-my-friend-so-and-so, bit. All I had to do was try to talk to them man-to-man, and I realized they weren't good enough."

"Dad, that's the thing. It's not up to you to decide who's good enough for me. That's my decision."

"This guy is from Tennessee, Tara. He doesn't even live here. He hasn't even been here in who knows how long. He's a nice guy, but I don't want him messing with you. I don't want you getting hurt."

"Can you just let me be the judge of what I'm doing, Dad? Can you trust me enough to know that I won't get hurt?"

Billy didn't answer. Trey assumed he must have answered her some other way. He was watching for shadows on the floor and poised to move just in case someone came into the locker room.

The next thing Billy said was, "Did Miguel keep his hands up today?"

"Most of the time. He was tired at the end, and started dropping them, but he's doing better."

"Okay. Thank you. Marvin's waving at you."

For a few seconds, Trey heard nothing else. The next thing he heard was footsteps and then he saw a shadow. It was with great haste that he tiptoed to the other side of the room, dropping his bag just in time to turn the sink on and pretend like he was washing his hands.

Billy.

It was Billy who came into the locker room several seconds later. "Just the man I was looking for," Billy said.

"Yes sir?"

"Come see me in my office before you leave, please."

"Okay, well, I was heading out now," Trey said.

"Okay, then come now. Wait for me outside and we'll walk over there together."

"Okay, yes sir," Trey said. He waited by the exit of the locker room. He could see Tara, near the front entrance talking to Marvin Jones, but he didn't go to her or try to get her attention. He just stood there, feeling nervous and thoughtful about what Billy would say.

"Come with me," Billy said. "I just wanted to ask you a few questions."

They walked along the edge of the gym until they reached the offices. Billy walked into the small office that had once been Marvin's but was now his. Trey followed him.

"Tara didn't know what it is your dad did besides real estate," Billy said.

"He owns commercial real estate in Nashville, and he's also got some land and property in Brentwood, where we live. He's an investor. I got into investing at a young age. I didn't know my great-grandmother who used to live across the street."

Trey took a deep breath, and Billy gestured for him to sit down. Instead of crossing to the other side of the desk to sit down across from Trey, Billy propped himself against his desk. He was so close to Trey that their legs were almost touching.

Trey swiveled to create a little distance.

"Do you believe in Jesus Christ our Lord and Savior, Mister Harper?"

"Yes sir."

"Have you ever been arrested?" Billy asked.

"No sir."

"Have you ever been married?"

"No sir."

"Okay, I'm going to make this as direct as I can," Billy said. "Tara is my first and only daughter. I didn't think I would be giving you this whole speech for a while, but she came in covered up today, and I knew something was going on."

"I'm afraid I'm lost," Trey said.

"My daughter came in this morning wearing those longer shorts and covering her legs up. Her shirt was different, too, bigger and baggier, and I knew something was going on."

"I would think you would want her to wear longer shorts," Trey said. He glanced at Billy's desk, at the family photos he had sitting in the corner.

"I do, but what I'm saying is that my daughter didn't realize she needed to cover herself up until she met you, Mister Harper. That might not mean much to you, but, to me, it means a lot. That's how innocent she is. She's just realizing that someone might want to look at her legs. What it implies is that Tara sees something new in you. You have to understand the significance of this and realize that Tara looks different than what she is."

Billy paused and looked at Trey, waiting to hear if he was paying attention.

"How so?" Trey asked.

"She looks tough. She boxes, and she hits like a guy. She's fast and tough and brave. She even seems really mature, and she is, she is mature, I'm not saying she's not, but Trey, she's also innocent. She's pure. She's trusting, and she's new to all this. I can see her acting a certain way about you. And I just don't want to see her get hurt." He paused but then continued. "So, if you're just being casual with her, you might as well just keep moving. Or at least keep your relationship to one of a normal landlord/tenant. I'm respectfully asking you to do that." Billy regarded Trey who just looked back at him.

"Okay," Trey said, finally.

"Okay what?" Billy asked.

"Okay, I would leave her alone, but I'm not being casual with Tara," Trey said, hoping and praying he was saying the right thing. He was nervous around Billy. "I'm honestly sitting here wondering what I can say to you to make you just snap and know what I'm thinking and feeling about her. I like her, Mister Castro. I really do. If I didn't like her so much, I'd probably give up on her by now because I'm so intimidated by you."

Billy laughed at that, and Trey let out a laugh since he was relieved at the sight of Billy laughing.

He would have to take to heart what Billy was saying. He was right, Tara was tough, but she was innocent, too. Trey was way more experienced with women than she was with men. He knew these things, and he knew he didn't want to hurt her, but Billy's warning carried weight, and Trey found himself reflecting on it for the next few days.

Chapter 15

Tara
Four days later

Trey had been quiet and thoughtful for the last few days. We had spent time together every day, and we had fun and got along great, but he was slightly introspective. We had kissed a few times, but it was restrained and didn't feel as passionate as that first night. After the way we acted that first night, I almost felt like we would go around announcing our love and being unable to keep our hands off of each other. But that was just a fantasy that had occurred in my own mind.

We had met at the gym three times this week, and we kept our distance to the point where my family assumed we were just friends or getting to know each other. We were obviously attracted to each other, but there was no blatant, public boyfriend/girlfriend thing going on like I thought there would be.

It was now Wednesday evening, and Trey would leave in a few days to go back to Nashville. He would be busy between now and then, entertaining a couple of friends from high school who were coming in to visit and see his property in Galveston.

I had just come home from Miss Gwendolyn's studio. I knew Trey's friends were coming over this afternoon, so it didn't surprise me when I climbed the stairs and heard noise and talking. I thought the television was on because I heard women's voices as well, but I couldn't tell if it was live or recorded.

The door to his apartment was open, and I did my best to sneak past it since I didn't want to interrupt.

"Tara!" Trey called my name as I walked past, and I turned and glanced into his apartment. There were tons of people, and I didn't feel prepared to walk into the room wearing sweatpants over a ballet leotard. I smiled and waved but kept walking.

"Tara." Trey came into the hallway, saying my name.

I had almost made it to my door by this time, and I turned and looked at Trey. I had seen him earlier this morning, but it was brief and he had changed clothes since then.

"Come in here," he said. "Please, just for a minute. Come meet everyone. Lee and Tyler are two of my oldest friends from school. I thought you'd want to come in here and meet them."

"Okay," I said nodding and beginning to walk toward him. I thought about going into my apartment to put my things away, but I opted to go straight over to him since he seemed to be waiting for me. I tried to act happy and confident as I came into the room.

"Everyone, this is Tara Castro. Tara, these are some of my good friends from Tennessee. This is Tyler and his girlfriend Cassie. That's Lee, and these two are Emily and Elizabeth."

Elizabeth. Beth from Mexico was the first thing that popped into my mind when Trey introduced her. I felt sick to my stomach, but I just smiled and greeted all of them. Vaguely, in the midst of the haze of jealousy and insecurity, I heard Trey saying something about my dance uniform.

"Yes, I'm just coming from the dance studio," I said, explaining my clothing. "I should be going so I can change and everything." I waved at them. "It was so nice meeting you all. I hope you have fun in Galveston."

There were five of them, and they all answered me with the various responses. They told me goodbye like it was no big deal at all, but I could see that Trey was looking at me closely and wondering why I was leaving so soon.

I smiled and reached out to hug him goodbye, kissing him briefly on the cheek.

"Don't leave," he said, whispering near my ear.

I pulled back, smiling at him. "I'm going to let you hang out with your friends," I said. I started to walk out with as little awkwardness as possible.

"Hey, I'm coming. I'll be back in just a minute," he announced to the others. He followed me into the hall, and I looked back at him once we were out there and couldn't be overheard. "Come hang out

149

with us," he said. "I didn't know so many people were coming. Tyler brought Cassie, and she wanted to bring her friends. They're only staying a couple of nights here before going to Austin. Cassie's grandparents own a ranch over there. They're making a whole trip of it. I had no idea."

"That's fine," I said. "I'm not mad or anything."

"They're going to stay downstairs, in the studio space," he added. "It's too many people for my apartment."

"Oh, yeah, of course."

"I figured it wouldn't matter to you since you weren't moving in yet."

"No, no it doesn't bother me at all," I said. "It's your building."

"Are you coming to hang out with us tonight?"

"No, I'm kind of tired after work. I'm going to let you catch up with your friends."

"I thought we had already said you were going to go out with us."

"We did, but I didn't know you had so many people, and I didn't know I'd be so tired. I had a long day."

"Are you sure?" he asked, looking disappointed.

"I'm sure," I said.

In the seconds of silence that followed I was extremely tempted to mention Beth. I wanted to ask him if it was the same person from Mexico. But I didn't. I was too scared he'd say it was.

"I've got the closet closed and locked downstairs," he said. "They won't go in there and even if they did they wouldn't find the trigger."

"I'm not worried about it," I said. "Please don't feel like you owe me an explanation."

There was definitely awkwardness between us.

"Okay," he said, not knowing how to take my last statement.

"My dad said you were going to the 10am workout tomorrow, so I guess I'll see you in the morning if you come to that."

"Okay," he said again.

It felt like Trey was confused, and honestly, I was confused, too. I went into my apartment feeling jealous and disappointed. I had plans to go out with Trey and his friends tonight, and now suddenly I wasn't doing that.

I had no idea why I said I wasn't going.

He wanted me to go.

If I didn't want him to be seduced by those women, I should have gone with him. I was frustrated with myself for staying home. I tried to tell myself I was relieved to get out of meeting five new people and making all that nervous conversation, but the truth of the matter was that I wished I had gone, and I beat myself up about it. I listened for noise all evening, but I didn't hear them come back.

I figured there was a chance they had come in quietly, but I wasn't sure. I went to bed at 11pm, and fell asleep at midnight reading a book I had read twice before.

I woke up to a strange sound.

It was a pinging sound, but it stopped as soon as I gained consciousness.

I looked at the clock.

It was 12:38am, and I blinked at the digital numbers, trying to make sense of my surroundings.

Ping.

It sounded like something hit my window.

Ping, ding, ding.

It had happened again, only this time something ricocheted. I listened closely, sleepily feeling like a logical assumption was hail. It happened again, *ping*, right on my window. I got out of bed and went over there, opening the curtains looking downward.

There was a group of people. Trey and all five of his friends were standing on the edge of the street, looking up at my window. Someone saw me open the curtain, and they cheered, and pointed at me. I blinked, feeling like I was in a dream.

Trey saw me and he waved. I was out-of-it, but I unlocked and opened the window by instinct.

"Come down here and come with us!" Trey called. "We're going over to the beach."

"Tonight?"

"Yes! Right now."

"I was sleeping," I said, blinking.

"You're not sleeping now!" another guy replied, causing a few people to laugh.

"Please," Trey said, raising his arms like he thought I might just jump out of the window.

"Okay, give me three minutes."

It was really more like five or six minutes, but I went from a dead sleep to dressed and leaving my apartment quicker than I had ever done in my life.

I instinctually put on an old faithful outfit—jeans and a t-shirt layered with a plaid button-down shirt and black Converse. I pulled my hair half-up and tried to adjust it some. I contemplated putting on a little makeup, but my face was still sensitive from sleeping, so I went without it.

Trey was waiting at my door when I walked out. He was standing there, smiling at me. I hadn't expected to see him there. I thought they were all waiting on me outside, and I was talking to myself when I walked out of my door.

"What did you say?" Trey asked.

"Oh, my gosh, I did not even see you there," I said, laughing a little as I turned to close the door.

"What were you saying?" he asked.

"I was just talking to myself," I said. "Thinking of how late it was and what time I had to be up in the morning."

"I'm sorry for waking you up," he said quietly. "But I wanted you with me."

I was about to turn to him with a smile when he said that, but just then, a girl walked out of his apartment, and my smile faded somewhat.

"Emily had to use the restroom and the working one downstairs was occupied."

"Elizabeth is still in there," she said gesturing to Trey's apartment. "I'm going outside with Tyler and them.

"We'll meet you out there," Trey said.

"I'm jealous," I whispered once Emily went down the steps.

"Of her using the restroom?" Trey asked.

"Shhh, no, but of them in general. I'm sure the Beth who's here is the same one from Mexico, and I'm telling myself that it's no big deal, but—"

"What? No, what are you even saying?"

"I thought this was the Beth who tried to kiss you in Mexico," I said.

He grinned. "Elizabeth? I guess that technically is the same name, but no. This is Elizabeth, that was Beth. They're two different women."

Elizabeth chose that moment to come out of Trey's apartment, and I could feel myself blush.

Chapter 16

I walked with Trey to his apartment door and waited next to him while he locked it. Elizabeth waited with us.

"Hi," I said to her, smiling and being nice as we both stood there.

"Hi," she said. "Galveston's awesome. I've never been here, so I didn't know what to expect."

I smiled at her as we started down the stairs. We went ahead of Trey.

"Thank you," I said. "I love my home."

"Trey said your dad is Easy Billy Castro," she said, as we walked. "My dad and grandpa are fans of his. I can remember them watching him fight on television when I was a kid."

"Yeah, thank you. My dad loves the sport. He still runs a gym right over there." By this time, we had opened the door from the apartments, and I gestured across the street to Bank Street Boxing.

"Oh, believe me, Trey already told us all about it," Elizabeth said.

"Told us about what?" Cassie asked. They were all standing on the sidewalk, close enough to the door so they were instantly a part of our conversation.

"About Tara, and her dad, and the boxing gym," Elizabeth said.

"Pfft, that's all he's talked about," Lee said. "I never dreamed he'd inherit a building in Texas and pick up boxing. This dude never ceases to amaze me."

A lot of people talked at once, commenting on Trey and his spontaneity.

"Are we driving or walking?" Tyler asked through the noise of the other comments.

"Let's drive," Trey said.

All seven of us got into Lee's van on our way to the beach. Trey and I ended up on a bench seat in the middle row with Emily. We had to squeeze-in tight to each other, which was absolutely no problem. The clock on the dash confirmed that it was nearly 1am, and I grinned feeling out-of-it and delirious in the best way possible. Trey put his arm around me and I leaned into him as we drove. I gave the driver, Lee, directions to a great parking spot on the seawall. We took our shoes off and left them in the van before we set off on our trek down the beach.

Trey reached out and took my hand the minute we started walking, and he didn't let go of me the whole time. I stayed close to him, feeling thankful for the constant contact. His friends were outgoing, and they were the type of people who had a lot going for them. They were young professionals who had ideas, and were smart, and made me feel challenged. Trey was proud of the business I would be opening soon, and he told them all about my plans. They were all friendly and easy to be around, and I was sad that I had wasted an evening being all worked up about it.

We walked for thirty minutes one way before Trey made the call to turn around. We talked on our way back but we took breaks in our conversation and listened to the sounds of the gulf.

"How was it growing up with Billy Castro as your dad?" Emily asked after a few seconds of silence. She had been the one to ask, but the whole group looked at me like they were all curious to hear my answer.

I sighed, trying to figure out how I should respond. "Well, the simple answer is that it was normal. I didn't know anything else. But I know what you're trying to ask. I mean, some kids' dads wear a suit and tie. Mine came home with bruises and sprains and battle scars. He's a physical guy, and he feels like he was created to be a warrior. He loves what he does. He's up at that gym almost every day, coaching and teaching the ones coming up through the ranks now."

"Is that you?" Tyler asked. "Are you moving up the ranks?"

"Me? No. I do box. I love it. I'm at the gym five days a week. I spar and everything, but I'm not trying to take a match. I have fun doing it, and it's great for self-defense, obviously."

"Trey better watch out," Lee said, teasing Trey.

"Trey doesn't get much of a struggle from me," I said.

Everyone whooped and reacted when I said that. It got way more of a reaction then I expected it to. All I meant was that Trey gave me no reason to use self-defense on him, but they took it like I was being flirty. I smiled along with them, but I was glad it was dark to hide the fact that I was blushing.

Trey pulled me closer as we walked. I was grateful for the contact, and I leaned into him.

"You said you had a little brother," Emily said. "What's the story with him? Is he a fighter like your dad?"

"Will? Yeah, definitely. Both of us have been at the gym learning how to box since we were barely big enough to fit into those little toddler boxing gloves. Will plays every sport, though. He tries to fit it all in. I don't know if he'll try to box professionally. I don't think he will. But he'll probably take a few amateur matches just to get the... life lessons, or whatever... that's what my dad says. He'll probably compete for a year in the golden gloves, just for the experience. My mom's not so sure. She hates seeing Will box or play football or any of that rough stuff."

"And then there's ballet?" Lee said. "What a combination."

"I can see how the two could go together," Emily said. "It seems like you need some grace to be a good boxer."

"Definitely," I agreed. "So many times, my father has used me and my ballet training as an example during class when he talks about form and footwork."

"I could be a boxing ballerina," Lee said.

"Is it still called a ballerina for a guy?" Trey asked.

"Yeah, do you call dudes ballerinas?" Lee asked. "Or is it ballerinos?" He said the word in a silly way.

Everyone laughed at him for making a funny joke, but I said, "It seriously is that."

"What? No. *Balleri-nos*? Are you serious?"

"Yes," I said. "Different companies refer to guys as different things. The French have a totally different name. Ballerina and ballerino are Italian, I think, but yes, a ballerino is a male dancer."

"That is hilarious!" Emily said, laughing at Lee.

"Did you have no idea?" I asked. "Surely, you must've heard it before and it was in the back of your mind."

"I promise, I have not heard of that. I just made it up. I can't believe that's really a thing. That is the funniest thing I've ever heard. Ballerino. I think I might be a genius."

"I think it's the ballerinos who are genius," Tyler said. "Think about it. They put themselves in this occupation where a bunch of beautiful ladies are climbing all over them and dancing around them all the time."

Trey looked at me with a scowl. "You're not climbing all over dudes, are you?"

"No," I said, laughing, but secretly loving that he would be jealous.

We made it back to the van and took a minute to dust off our feet and organize some shells we had found. Emily had never been to the beach and she was the most excited about her shells. She had a box in the back of the van which she brought to the front so that she could set out her treasures. I turned to the side, facing Trey to give her room to put her box between us. I was the one who offered to scoot over and make room. She could have found a different solution for her shells, but I was glad to have the excuse to face Trey and get closer to him on the way home.

I was facing him and holding his hand, and my blood ran warm as a result of our contact. Everyone talked, and we chimed in, but I could hardly concentrate on anything other than the place where my skin touched Trey's.

Because of how we were positioned, Trey had full access to my arm. He took my hand and placed it, palm down on his stomach, holding it there. He was wearing a thin shirt, and I could easily feel the warmth of his skin and the taut ridges of his abs.

He acted like tucking my hand there was an absentminded move on his part. But it was more than that. You don't just let someone touch your stomach. I knew that from boxing. It was a vulnerable place. He was leaving himself fully exposed, letting me touch the soft spot. Maybe I was making too much of it, but goodness.

His hand holding my hand and trapping it on his stomach—it gave me all sorts of ooey gooey feelings. Lee was driving, and he basically knew how to get back to the apartment on Bank Street. He asked me about one turn, but otherwise he knew.

They had already mentioned that the guys were going to sleep upstairs in Trey's apartment while the girls slept downstairs. They were prepared and were traveling with some cot mattresses, but I thought about offering them my apartment since I had two couches and a chair.

I almost invited the girls to stay with me, but I thought I might regret getting swept away in the moment. I had fun with them tonight, but I wasn't sure if I was up for getting myself into two days of company in my apartment. I went with my gut and kept my mouth shut about it, but I told myself that I would ask Trey about it when we were alone and make sure he knew I didn't mind having his friends stay with me.

For now, it was late, and everyone needed to get to bed. They had it worked out. I figured I could maybe mention it to Trey later, and they could stay with me tomorrow night.

Chapter 17

We left the girls downstairs, and I walked upstairs with the guys. I told Trey goodnight with the rest of them. We didn't make a big deal about it since Lee and Tyler were there. I kissed his cheek quickly and told him that I'd still be going to the gym in the morning.

He said he would be there, and I took off down the hall, quietly saying goodnight to the other two. I looked over my shoulder as I was about to unlock my door. Trey had just opened his door.

"Hey Trey."

He looked over his shoulder at me.

"Don't let me forget to ask you something about downstairs."

I saw him tell his friends that he would be back. They went into his apartment, and he turned and came my way. He walked toward me, smiling and looking straight at me. I had to stop myself from wiggling with excitement.

"Hey, I wanted to tell you... your friends are welcome to stay in my apartment if they'd be more comfortable. The girls, I mean."

Trey smiled and pulled me right inside the door to my apartment. He closed the door most of the way and took me into his arms. He just held me tightly like he was never going to let me go.

"What happened?" I asked. "What changed?"

"What do you mean?" he asked.

"You. Tonight. Something's different with you. Something changed. All week, we weren't holding hands in front of people or anything, and tonight, we were glued together."

I spoke quietly even though we were alone. I was being vulnerable and saying things that made me feel shy. I stared at his shirt—at the top of his chest near his collar.

"I wanted to be glued to you all along," he said. "I was trying to slow down and be patient."

"Why would you want to do something like that?" I asked, softly, playing with him, flirting.

"Your dad."

"What did he do?"

"It's not bad, he just pulled me aside and reminded me that I needed to be patient. I just wanted to go as slow as you needed."

Sheer mortification washed over me when Trey said those words. I felt a whooshing sensation of dread and embarrassment.

"What? Did he actually tell you that?"

"It's not bad, Tara. Don't be mad at him. It's the truth that I need to take your feelings seriously. And I do. I feel serious about you, and I'm not trying to go too fast or hurt you. All week, I've just been thinking about it and trying to figure out where to go from here."

I let out a frustrated sigh. I was so mad.

"I cannot believe my dad," I said, dazedly.

"Don't be mad at him," Trey said, holding me closer. "He loves you. He's just trying to protect you."

I pulled back and let my eyes meet his—our brown eyes connecting like they had done countless times.

"Thank you for not letting that run you off," I said.

"I won't. Ultimately, I'm my own man. But the things he said, they did make me check myself, you know? I've really been evaluating my long-term thoughts—where I see myself in the future and what I hope to get out of all this with you."

He held onto me gently, his arms resting comfortably on my sides.

"And what is it you see in your future?" I asked.

"You, Tara. You're the thing I want. Not the building or any number of buildings. I don't even care about living in a certain city. I want you in my life, and that's all."

I let my arms rest on him, holding onto him.

"Being with those people tonight, having my Nashville people here, it reminds me of what's back home. And no offense, they're great, they're all great people. But being with them just makes me know how badly I wanted you. I'm trying to be next to you. I feel like everything I could want is here."

I felt weak in the knees. "I'm going to tell my dad that I'm with you and that's final," I said. "If he says anything else to you, please come tell me about it."

"He's fine," Trey said. "He and I will be fine. You don't need to go take up for me with your dad."

"I thought about that," I said. "But I will, if you need me to."

He gave me a squeeze. "I can take care of Billy Castro... *easy*." He said it just the right way that it was a play on my dad's nickname, and I smiled at his joke. He leaned down and kissed me. His mouth was firm and warm, and I had not been able to kiss him enough during the last few days. I felt deprived of his kiss, and it made me lean into him.

He pulled me close, turning to the side, and kissing me deeply. Oh gosh, his kiss. Ohhhhhhh. He had never, ever kissed me like this. His tongue came into my mouth, and the silky intrusion gave me a completely different feeling than the gentle kisses we shared up until now. I held on and let him kiss me deeply, leaning into him, feeling like I might melt.

Trey held the back of my head, kissing me expertly for several long, hazy minutes. It was the middle of the night, and those moments felt fevered and dreamlike. All we did was stand there in my doorway and kiss. We were on our feet, and yet it was intense, like his kiss caused me to leave my own body.

I was awe-struck when Trey finally pulled back. He broke the kiss, but then he kissed me again, twice

165

and then three times. I smiled when he pulled back for the last time. He had a hold of my face, and I could feel that my smile caused me to get chubby cheeks. He smiled at the sight of that and leaned in to kiss my mouth again.

Our lips were wet from kissing, and it felt like a cool, sweet stamp of heaven when he did it.

"I better go," he whispered reluctantly, staring at me.

"I know. Your friends are waiting for you."

He leaned in and kissed me again. "I'm sorry for waking you up," he said. He was still holding me close, not moving, his mouth was only inches from mine, even when he pulled back.

I smiled at his comment about waking me up. "Are you sorry?" I asked sarcastically.

"No. I'm not. This is, by far, the best part of my day. I'm not sorry at all. But I'm sorry if you're tired at work tomorrow. That, I would be sorry about."

"I'm sure I'll survive," I said. (Kiss.) "It was worth it," I added. (Kiss. This one was longer. This was one where he sucked gently on my lower lip.) I was barely able to breathe, much less form a sentence. "Are you going to be at class at ten?" I asked, finally. (Kiss.)

"Yes," he answered. "I'll see you in a few hours."

***

Of course, my thoughts ran wild and it was difficult to get to sleep, even after my head hit the pillow. It was ridiculously late when I finally fell asleep. I set the alarm for the last possible minute. I got out of bed and went to my father's gym, feeling puffy and unrested. My eyes burned and went to the coaches lounge where I poured a quarter of a cup of coffee, added cream and sugar, and drank it down without taking time to savor it.

I didn't care about being tired. I was in the best mood possible, considering how little sleep I got. I drank down some coffee and chewed a mint on my way out of the lounge.

Trey made it to class.

I saw him from across the gym as I came out of the back. He was in a group, talking to my dad and two other people. They were smiling, and I went toward them.

It ended up being a big morning class. My dad didn't usually teach on Saturday mornings, and it seemed that word had gotten out that he would be here because there were about double the number of people we normally had.

I tried to make my way over to Trey, but Miguel stopped me to ask me a question, and by the time I answered it, my father was starting class.

We did warmups, and all of us were sweating by the time those were finished. My dad did not mess around when he was running a class, and he went straight into drilling after warmups.

"Grab a partner!" Dad called. "One of you get pads, the other put on your gloves."

I instantly went to Miguel. I didn't even hesitate since I knew that working with him had been part of my job description lately. I glanced at Trey who had partnered with Greg, one of our heavyweights.

My dad and Coach Dizzy came up to Miguel and me while we were still finding a spot on the mat. "Miguel, I'm going to get Dizzy to hold pads for you today," Dad said, handing the older coach some equipment.

Dad looked at me. "Come with me," he said, and we started walking. "I want you to come partner-up with this guy over here. Show him around."

By the time Dad finished talking, he and I were on our way to the other side of the mat. Trey could see that we were headed toward him, and he watched us approach. "Greg, come over here and rotate with Tyson and Mark. Or better yet, go with Brandon." Greg nodded and took off. "Trey, I wanted to get you to partner up with my daughter, Tara. She's going to work with you today."

This was the type of introduction my dad made all the time. I worked with new members a lot. I smiled and stood opposite Trey, both of us squaring off in loose but athletic stances.

"I guess you're my partner," I said.

"I guess so," he said.

"Is that okay?" I asked.

A smile was Trey's only response, but we both knew he thought it was okay.

"Our first combination is going to be jab, jab, cross, hook, cross. Nice and easy. Five punches. Watch your foot work. Stay light on your feet. Get your rhythm, stay loose. And *keep your hands up, people*... ready, and... go.

"Jab, jab, then what was after that?" Trey asked.

"Jab, jab, hook, cross, hook. No. Cross, hook, cross."

Trey threw the first punch.

"Jab with the other hand," I said, smiling.

He smiled at himself, and then he did it again.

"That's right," I said.

"Sorry," he said, doing the combination slowly. "You make me nervous."

"Don't be sorry, and don't be nervous. Just get a rhythm. *Jab, jab, hook,* yes, now *cross,* good, *hook,* yes! Great, Trey. You're really good. You have good instincts."

We went through several sets of the combination—all while moving around and trying to stay light on our feet. Trey was not trying to show me his strength. I could tell he was strong, but if he was trying to show me anything, it was his precision.

He was new to boxing and he wasn't very technical compared to the veterans, but he was amazing for someone who had only been to a few classes. He was smooth, and he was confident, and he had great natural athleticism.

We were doing two-minute rounds, and near the end of it, Trey got tired and dropped his hands. I reached out and tapped him on the cheek lightly with the palm of my pad.

He laughed, knowing that I could have punched him right then.

"Keep your hands up," I reminded him.

He finished the round breathing heavy but smiling. My dad went into a speech about keeping our core centered and our feet under us to retain a constant center of balance. He used me and my ballet as an example again, posing in something close to an arabesque. He was a dynamic teacher and he had everyone laughing.

He gave us another combination, and we went to work again. This one was longer, but Trey kept up, taking it slowly and not freaking out and trying to go hard like most new people would.

"What time do you get off work?" he asked between rounds.

"Four," I said. I knew his friends were still in town tonight and that we were all planning on going out to eat.

"Cassie has a video projector," he said. "She was talking about it yesterday. I was thinking we could rent a movie and watch it on the wall of the studio— I think it can go up to like ten feet wide."

"Oh, that would be amazing," I said. "What movie?"

"I don't know. I haven't even brought it up with anyone else. I just remember her saying she had that projector, and I was feeling like watching a movie with my girlfriend, so I was hoping to make that happen."

"Is she me?" I said, feeling giddy.

He didn't get to answer before the bell rang. Dad gave us a long, eight-punch combination to perform. Trey did the first part and then looked at me. "Jab, uppercut, hook, cross," I added when he paused.

He did the four remaining punches.

"Yes, she's you," he said, continuing our conversation. "I want to watch a movie with you after dinner tonight. But also, one more thing." We paused while he performed the combination.

"What?" I asked.

"Meet me in the room later" he said. "For a couple of minutes. I know we're eating dinner together and the movie, but we're not going to get a minute alone. Just meet me in the room for like two minutes." He did the first part of the combination, but he hesitated.

"Jab, uppercut, hook, cross," I said when he paused, and he delivered the rest of the combination. We had to fit in our conversation between all this work and give no clue to my father that we were talking and scheming.

"You name a time and I will be in there," I said. "I usually get home by four, and I just need to take a quick shower. Do we just use the roof since your friends are in the rooms?"

"Yes. I'm going to use the roof access, too," he said "Jab, uppercut, hook, cross." He was the one to say the end of the combination this time, and I smiled that he remembered.

"They want to go back to the beach today, but we should be back by four. Can you meet me upstairs when you get off work? Maybe at four fifteen?"

I smiled and nodded. "I can't wait."

Chapter 18

I thought I would beat Trey to the secret room.

I got off of work a little early, and freshened up. I found my way onto the roof and down to the secret room by a minute or two before four o'clock. I was fifteen minutes early, so I was shocked to find Trey in there.

"*What?*" I said as I came down the new spiral stairs. "What are you doing here so early?"

"I'm waiting for you," he said.

He was sitting in the chair, sprawled out, confidently messing with a toy. It looked like a black rubber ball, and he might as well have been a rock star, sitting there, tossing it casually.

"I was going to get down here first and wait for you," I said.

"Well, I beat you to it," he said.

He stood up, tossing the ball into the corner of the chair before turning just in time to catch when I walked into his arms.

"What's that ball?" I asked.

"Just a racquetball," he said. "I found it in Lee's van. I've been messing with it all afternoon."

He took me into his arms, burying his face in my neck, kissing me lightly, hugging me and holding onto me gently.

"You smell so good," I said.

"You smell good," he replied.

"Not as good as you." I sniffed his hair.

"I just took a shower when we got home from the beach. There was barely any hot water. They've taken over all of my space."

"Not *all* of your space," I said, referring to this room and raising my eyebrows a little.

"You're right," he said. "That's why I told you to meet me here. Because in front of them it's hard to find an opportunity to..." he trailed off and leaned in, letting his lips softly touch mine for a heart-stopping second before pulling back.

"I know," I said, holding onto him. "We're going to be eating dinner and watching a movie, and everyone will be right there, so it'll be hard to find time to..."

I kissed him again, and he smiled.

Our contact was torturously gentle, but finally he grabbed a hold of the sides of my sweatshirt, pulling me in. He gave me a little tug as he began to move. "Come sit by me for a minute," he said.

I retrieved the small black ball out of the corner of the chair and then stepped back to let Trey sit down. I slipped off my shoes before sitting on the arm of the chair, letting my legs drape across his lap and tucking my feet next to him. Trey rested his arm on my ankles, and I fiddled with the ball.

"Thank you for meeting me up here," he said in a sweet, patient tone. "I wanted a few minutes with my girl. I imagined those guys would be doing their

174

own thing while they were here, but everyone's been around a lot, wanting to hang out."

"They're nice though," I said.

"Yeah," he agreed. "It's fine. They're pretty easy, but they're around all the time."

"They'll be leaving tomorrow, right?" I asked, since I was uncertain.

"Yes, but then I just have one more night before I have to go back to Nashville again."

I made a disappointed noise. "Let's not talk about it," I said, tucking my head next to him. I was dreading it that much—I didn't want to think about it or mention it. I knew he had to go back, but I was doing my best not to acknowledge it. *If I didn't acknowledge it, it didn't exist, right?*

"How was work?" Trey asked.

"It was good," I said. "Jesse came by."

"Your friend from high school?"

"Yeah. I told her I was going to be opening the studio, and she said she'd be willing to teach a class or two for me now that she's home from school."

I thought back to my conversation with Jesse earlier that day. I hadn't talked to her in a while, and she didn't know about my relationship with Trey. I told her I was seeing someone, and she asked so many questions that she figured out that it was the same guy she saw in the diner the day I first met him. She joked with me, saying that I was mean for going after 'her man'. I had laughed it off at the time, but the more I thought about her comments, the more annoyed I got. I thought back to my conversation with her, hoping I had done enough to let her know he was actually my man.

"Did you hear me?" Trey asked as I was lost in thought.

"No. What'd you say?"

He laughed. "You're so spaced out."

"I know. I was thinking about talking to Jesse."

"It's cool that she's going to help you out," he said.

"Yeah. Is that what you said?"

"No. I was looking at your legs, and I asked you where you got those calves. It's like little rocks in there. Is that from ballet?"

"And boxing," I said, looking at my own calves. With the way my legs were positioned across him, my muscles were somewhat flexed. I peered down and saw what he was looking at. There was a line on my calf along the ridge of my muscle. He cupped his hand around that area and I flexed even more, causing his face to light up.

He smiled mischievously at me. "You seriously are a little dynamo."

"Ooh, I like that name. Dynamo. That'll be my nickname if I ever take a fight."

"I thought you weren't planning on fighting," he said.

"I'm not," I said, smiling and assuring him. "But if any nickname could tempt me to do it…"

I trailed off, and he laughed.

"How was the beach?" I added.

"It was good. The girls got sunburned—especially Emily. They put on a bunch of suntan oil and laid out in their bikinis all day. The only time they moved was to flip over. When I left them downstairs, they were pretty miserable, rubbing aloe vera on each other."

I just stared at him, nodding wryly. "So, you spent the day with a bunch of oiled-up women in bikinis. That's just great..." I said, sarcastically.

He smiled and gave me a reassuring squeeze. "I hardly saw them. We went surfing. Tyler really wanted to try it, so we rented boards. We were in the water the whole time."

"Surfing? Really? Were you any good?"

"I wasn't *good*," he said. "I've never even tried it before, so I can't say I was good. I did get up on the board several times, though. I think I could get the hang of it, eventually. We met some guys at the surf shop who went out with us. The waves weren't big, but it was fun. Tyler and Lee are already talking about coming back so they can do it again. They'll get a hotel, but they love Galveston. They already have two restaurants they want to eat at all the time, and now surfing."

"I could see you being a surfer," I said. "You look like a surfer."

"You think so?" he asked.

I nodded. I cut my eyes toward the new trap door on the wall. "I can't believe everybody's right there and they have no idea this room even exists."

Trey smiled at that. "It's cool, huh?"

"The coolest."

"You're the coolest," he said. "And your dad partnered us up today," he added. "What's up with that?"

"I don't know. It surprised me, too. I thought maybe he just wanted Miguel to work with someone else. You were good, though. You did great." I smiled and bit my lip shyly, absentmindedly gazing at the curves of the side of his face.

"Do you know it's incredibly... attractive... that you know how to do that."

"That I know how to box?" I asked, letting out a little disbelieving laugh.

"Yes," he said, looking at me like he couldn't believe that I couldn't believe it.

"Well, thank you," I said. "That's one skill I never thought would come in handy when I'm trying to impress a man."

"You *didn't*?" he asked, his voice comically disbelieving.

I laughed. "No, I actually didn't," I said.

I touched the side of his jaw where he had some short, soft facial hair. I appreciated this moment for what it was—pure bliss. Those few minutes in his arms in our secret room were special and surreal. Maybe it was my rebellious side coming out, but

178

there was something fun about sneaking around and being unseen—being somewhere you're not supposed to be.

We went onto the rooftop on our way back to our respective apartments. We saw some pigeons up there, and Trey told me they were rock pigeons. "The ancestral kind," he said. I had no idea what that meant, so I asked him.

"They got brought to North America when it was colonized," he said. "The ones with bright feathers like this, the purple and green, they're from the line of those first brought over. Rock pigeons are feral now, and they come in a ton of dull colors, but these bright ones are from the ancestral line."

I nodded thoughtfully, thinking about pigeons. "Are pigeons and doves the same thing?" I asked. "I always thought they looked alike."

"Basically," he said. "Same family. Pigeons are bigger."

We were speaking quietly as we descended the staircase from the roof. I honestly had no idea how I was hopelessly smitten by the oddest things, like his ability to tell me facts about pigeons.

"Thank you, Professor," I said as we got to the bottom of the stairs.

I stood there and waited for him. Neither of us reached for the door handle. It was locked from the other side, and we were technically still in our secret space.

He grinned at me. "Are you making fun of me for knowing about rock pigeons?"

"No," I said. "On the contrary. I was thinking about how happy I am that you're so smart."

He leaned against the wall, pulling me in, holding me for one last minute.

"Tell me something else about birds," I said.

"They fly."

"Very funny," I said.

"No, I will, I'll tell you something. Let me think. Okay, male cardinals are so aggressive and territorial that they've been known to fight their own reflections in mirrors."

"Really?"

"Yes," he said, giving me an irresistible smile.

"How is it that being a big science nerd is unbelievably handsome?" I said. "It's like you being attracted to me with me boxing."

He laughed. "This is not at all the same as you boxing. That actually really is hot. You physically look beautiful doing it."

"Well, you look beautiful being smart," I said. "I feel like I could learn about rock pigeons all day."

He laughed. "I'm afraid I don't have a day of information on them," he said. "I pretty much gave you all I had already."

I smiled at him. "You're handsome, anyway, science or no science. I almost had to judo toss my friend Jesse today because she remembered you from the diner and couldn't stop talking about how fine you were."

"You and your friend talked about me?"

"Yes."

"What'd you say?"

"That you were mine," I said.

"No, you didn't," he said, smiling and teasing me.

"Yes, I did. Basically. I hope I did. I meant to."

He stared into my eyes. Both of us knew he had to get back to his friends.

"I'll see you at dinner," I said.

We broke apart, and I reached for the door handle, but he leaned in and kissed me. I kissed him back, but I was smiling because I was already in motion, opening the door.

And to my utter surprise, there was Tyler, standing in the hallway. He hadn't seen us kissing, but boy, was it close.

"Oh, hey," I said as soon as I saw him. My heart pounded. I didn't know what to say next. Trey was behind me, but he didn't hesitate.

"So that's where the circuit breaker is," he said to me as he came into the hallway. He closed the door, casually checking the lock. "This closet stays locked, but I'll get you a key in case that ever happens again."

I already had a key to this door, but I knew Trey was just trying to maintain the secrecy of the room, so I just smiled and nodded and thanked him.

"I'll see you at dinner," he said.

Chapter 19

Trey
Later that evening

Trey was a goal-setter, a real go-getter. He was accustomed to making moves and going after the things he wanted. It was an attitude that had served him well thus far. There was a certain compelling feeling he got when there was something he really wanted, and he felt that way about Tara. It was just unacceptable to think about moving forward without her as a fixture in his life. She added energy and vitality to the actual atmosphere, and Trey was basically addicted to it. Now that he had gotten used to having Tara around, he felt like he might not be able to breathe without her.

They ate dinner with his friends from Nashville. Tara introduced them to an Italian place that had a wood burning pizza oven. They talked about all sorts of things at dinner. Trey's friends told a few stories about old times, but Tyler and Lee were excited about their experience surfing, and they ended up talking a lot about their day at the beach and their trip to Galveston in general. They all agreed that they'd be sad to leave tomorrow.

The whole group went to rent a movie. Tara was the only one who had a membership at the store, so they just put the movie on her account. They rented an action movie with Keanu Reeves, mainly because it had surfing in it and the boys were officially obsessed with surfing now. Tara and Trey had both seen the movie before, most or all of them had, but they didn't care.

Cassie and Tyler set up the projector and got the movie ready. Elizabeth went with Trey and Tara to retrieve more blankets and cushions from upstairs so that they could make a comfortable viewing surface. Emily and Lee were in charge of opening and preparing the snacks, and within ten minutes, the studio had been transformed to a movie theater— something even better than a movie theater.

They piled up pillows, and sprawled out, making themselves comfortable and making sure everyone else could see. Trey was sprawled out, propped on a pillow, and Tara was sitting cross-legged next to him. She sat close enough that their legs brushed against each other.

"What's Harper going to do once he gets back to Nashville and can't go to his boxing class anymore?" Tyler asked.

"I'm wondering what he's going to do without surfing," Lee said.

Cassie nodded. "It's going to be hard to leave his second home in paradise."

Tara looked at Trey when they said that about him, and he stared back at her.

"I'm thinking I'll just hang on to that apartment upstairs instead of renting it out," he said. "That way, I can come anytime I want."

"I think you totally should," Emily said. "This building is so cool. Galveston's so cool. If I had this set up, and I could afford it, I'd definitely keep an apartment."

Trey kept his eyes on Tara. "I probably will," he said, staring at her. She regarded him with a challenging expression, and he regarded her right back.

"Did you see that fight with your dad and Mick Neilson?" Tyler said.

Tara broke eye contact with Trey to look at Tyler. They had talked to Tara a little about boxing, but they had been low-key about asking her about it.

"Were you at that fight?" he asked. "I mean, I just remember that so vividly. Your dad was just hit like so many times, and then, like all of a sudden..." (Tyler started shadow boxing.) "He was like bam, bam, bam, bam, bam. Just going at it. That was a championship match."

"I remember that match," Lee said.

"I know what you're talking about," Tara said. "But the only reason I remember that match is because so many people have brought it up and talked about it since it happened. Every match seemed the same to me at the time. We traveled with Dad, but Will and I stayed in a hotel with Mom and didn't even go to the venues. This was during my early childhood, before we could make the choice that we wanted to start going. Until then, Mom stayed back with us and we waited for Dad at the hotel. We would usually be asleep by the time he came in. I remember being aware of him winning sometimes and losing some, too. But my parents just got through all of them, win or lose, with a steady sort of reaction that made me feel like my dad's job was the most normal life ever."

"Well, coming from a guy whose parents are *actually* normal, no, I'd say having Easy Billy Castro for a dad is not normal at all. I was eating TV dinners while this girl was at Madison Square garden watching her dad fight in front of a million people."

Everyone laughed at Tyler, even Tara.

"It's funny how you see your life so differently than other people see it," she said, shaking her head.

"I'm pressing play!" Cassie announced from the back of the room.

"Who's hungry?" Emily asked.

"I'm still full from dinner," Elizabeth said.

Tara used all this distraction to move. She got onto her back, settling into a comfortable spot propped on a pillow next to Trey. He moved her, repositioning her pillow so that his arm was tucked beneath it. This meant she was now lying right beside him where their bodies were making contact at several places. It was the closest they had been all night, and Trey felt a current of warm electricity in his body as a result of being so close to her.

She was a catch. Trey had never thought of a person as a catch, but there was no other way to describe Tara. He felt like she was such a catch that if he didn't reel her in and keep her for himself, someone else would. He just couldn't stand by and let that happen.

He reached over and took her hand at the thought, and she held onto him, turning toward him a little and stretching up to speak to him quietly.

"I had fun tonight," she said. Her mouth was close to his ear, and she was speaking so quietly that there was no way anyone else heard her. Her voice tickled Trey's ear, and he closed his eyes, shutting out the movie and everything around him so that he could hear her, feel her. He lifted his chin to speak to her when she finished.

"What?" he asked, even though he had heard her the first time.

"I said I had so much fun with you tonight," she said, still whispering.

Her whisper caused a physical reaction in him. He moved to speak to her again. "Why are you saying that already?" he asked. "The night's not over."

She leaned up to speak next to his ear. This conversation was all happening slowly and quietly because they didn't want to disturb anyone.

"I know, but we might be rushed saying goodnight, and I just wanted you to know that I had fun. I like being your date."

Her voice in his ear.

It made Trey's heart race so fast his chest felt like it might explode. He caught himself holding her hand tightly, and he loosened his grip.

Tara knew he was affected by her mouth next to his ear, so she continued, "Also, you're great at boxing. I'm glad we partnered-up today. That was fun. You did so good."

Maybe it was her voice or her breath on his ear but she was driving him wild. Trey could see the images on the wall and hear the action, but was not even aware that there was a movie going on.

After a minute, he leaned down to speak to her. "Thank you," he whispered. "Billy Castro's daughter is my girlfriend, so I'm pretty much a natural."

Tara has been stoic during all of this whispering, but her chest shook with a few silent giggles when he said that.

She stretched up put her mouth next to his ear again. "You are seriously a natural," she said. "Unless you're just that anxious to try to impress me."

"That's probably the case, actually," Trey said.

She stretched to speak to him again. "Your breath tickles my ear when you talk."

He leaned in to whisper back to her. "What do you think I'm dealing with over here? I'm about ready to ditch these people and watch a movie upstairs."

"Just pretend you're interested," she said, whispering to him and looking at the side of his face as he pretended to watch the movie. "It'll be our little secret that we're talking. They'll all think we're paying attention."

Tara's voice traveled into Trey's ear in tones that must have been intentional because Trey had never been affected by a woman's voice like this before. The whispering. Gosh. He could feel the gentle puffs of air on his ear. Tara was an expert whisperer. And she was sweet. She said kind words to him that made him feel like he wanted her to always be his and only his.

Chapter 20

Tara

I had to go to work at the gym the following morning, so I missed Cassie, Tyler, and the rest of the crew from Nashville when they took off. I saw them getting into the van, but I was in the middle of mopping and couldn't get away. I had told them goodbye last night, anyway.

"Are you doing the class at noon?" Dad asked.

"I doubt it," I said. "I'm gonna take off in a minute. Trey's leaving for Nashville in the morning, so we'll probably hang out as much as possible today."

"Oh, Trey? Really? Because he was coming here for that class."

My head snapped up and I stared at my father, who laughed at my surprise.

"He just did class yesterday," I said.

"Well, I've done class every day for about twenty-five years."

"No, I'm just saying. I didn't think Trey had plans to come here today. I told him I was coming in for a couple of hours this morning, but after that we were going to—"

"I called him," Dad said, cutting me off.

"You called him?" I asked, wavering on being happy and mortified.

My dad grinned at me. "Yes."

"What did he say? What did you say?"

My dad was getting a kick out of my curiosity, I could tell. "I told him that he should come up here to do the workout at noon. Your mom will be here, so I thought he might want to come by and meet her."

I smiled and squinted at him. "Are you joking with me right now?"

"No. I'm one hundred percent serious. Why?"

"Because. How did you call him? How did you even get his number?"

"He filled out all kinds of stuff when he joined the gym. I have his phone number, his address, probably even his social security number."

"Do you?"

"No, but I do have a telephone number and I seriously did call him. Your mom's coming by. She and I were talking, and she said she hadn't met your friend, so I—"

"I was going to see if he wanted to go by the house this afternoon," I said. "Or maybe even eat dinner with y'all tonight."

Dad shrugged. "Well, I guess she'll get to meet him twice, because they'll both be here at noon."

Of course, I stuck around. I was obviously going to be there when Trey came. My mom got to the gym first, and within minutes, Trey walked in.

I went toward the door to meet him. He was looking handsome in athletic shorts and a t-shirt with a duffle bag draped over his shoulder.

"Hey," I said, when I got close enough for him to hear me.

"Hey," he said.

"My mom's here," I added, looking slightly apologetic since I didn't want him to feel bombarded.

"Good. I hope so. That's why your dad told me to come."

"I hope it wasn't weird that he called you," I said quietly.

"Not at all," he answered, smiling.

But we weren't alone anymore. My mom crossed over to us. I could tell Trey had made eye contact with her by the way his face changed. He grinned at her as she walked up.

"Hello," she said, moving past me for the hug.

"Hello," Trey said, pushing his bag behind him and reaching out to hug her back.

"I'm Tess Castro, Tara's mom."

"Tara's told me a lot about you," Trey said. "And I really like your paintings. I saw the ones in Tara's place, and I've seen a few others around town. There's one in the hardware store. I was staring at it just the other day. Really great stuff. I'd love to buy a piece sometime."

"Oh, of course," Mom said. "And thank you."

I watched them interact, feeling more nervous than ever. My heart was pounding, and I constantly wanted to cut in, but I just stood there and watched.

"Tara's excited about renting that jewelry store," Mom said.

"I'm excited to see what she'll do with it. She's going to make it beautiful. She already has."

"Oh, wow," my mom said, stunned by his sweetness. She blinked rapidly the way she does when she's about to tear up. "What do you think about God, Trey?"

"Mom!"

"No, it's okay," Trey said, laughing a little as he shook his head. "What do you mean?" he asked my mom.

"I mean do you know Him?"

"Yes ma'am, and Mister Castro asked me the same thing. That was basically the first thing he ever asked me."

"Seriously?" Mom asked, glancing proudly at Dad who was standing across the room.

"But Tara had already talked to me about it before either of you did. She and I talked about that, and, yes, I do. And I like that it's important to all of you. I respect that about you guys—that you just came out and asked me. Yes, I do know God. I think He had a hand in leading me here."

My mom was steady blinking, holding her eyes wide to dry them out so that she wouldn't cry. She went in and hugged Trey again. "Tara's so talented, and she's got great things ahead of her, but honestly, nothing makes me prouder of her than what you just said. If she remembers one thing we taught her..." Mom paused and took a deep breath, but then continued. "So, thank you. And thank you for all you're doing with that building. It's so nice to see it getting all fixed-up over there. And Tara can't wait to move in. Thank you for making that possible."

"It's m-my pleasure," Trey said, seeming like those weren't quite the words he was looking for.

"Billy's trying to get y'all started," Mom said, noticing my dad on the other side of the gym. We turned and saw that Dad was gesturing for us. "Tara said she might bring you by the house tonight," Mom added.

"Yes, ma'am, I hope so," Trey said.

Mom smiled and waved at us, and we took off to meet my dad. I held eye contact with her after Trey had already turned around, and she made a face at me. It was a serious, wide-eyed, intense expression that made me smile. I knew she loved him. For goodness sake, she had almost cried twice in the same number of minutes.

"I'm going to stick around for a little while!" Mom yelled. "I might be here when you're done."

"Okay!" I yelled back.

She was excited and curious, and I knew she was going to watch the class just to get a look at Trey.

The wonderful thing was that Trey didn't seem to care. He knew everyone at that gym was

194

scrutinizing and/or judging him on my behalf, and he walked right into it.

I partnered with a brand-new guy named Sam, and Dad put on pads and went with Trey. Dad was in a good mood, and he was teasing Trey in a way that made me know he liked him.

I could hear them a little during the class, but unfortunately Sam (an older guy who said he wanted to be a boxer his whole life) talked non-stop. He did what Dad instructed, and he swung for the fences when he did hit, but he worked slow enough that he was able to carry on a conversation the whole time.

I was not like that. I was not accustomed to talking during class. I answered him with short answers, and I tried to keep us on track as much as possible.

I didn't get to see Trey and my dad much at all. I could hear them some of the time, but Sam was a handful, and I was busy working with him. We were doing a particular combination toward the end of class that had us moving around some more. My dad and Trey ended up next to us. Trey was the one performing the drill, and I was aware of their rhythm, which was faster and smoother than mine and Sam's.

My dad made three guttural noises in a row as he lunged forward. He delivered blows—hard, fast slaps with the pads. I stopped what I was doing with Sam just to see what was going on. Trey blocked and shifted out of the way of my dad's counter.

195

"Ooh, that was good," Dad said, laughing. "You got hit with that yesterday."

Trey smiled. "I know. I remember. It hurt. That's why it didn't happen today."

"Good man," Dad said.

I turned to Sam, catching his sequence of punches. He wasn't able to hurt me because I knew what I was doing and I was able to avoid the full power of his follow-through. He would go slow, and take time between each combo, but when he hit, he hit hard. He weighed a hundred pounds more than I did, and he was hitting pads like he had something to prove.

I could handle it, though. My dad was aware of us, and he would deal with it if Sam got out of line. Plus, I would simply quit if I thought he was being too rough. I had done that more than once—just stopped and refused to go with someone. Anyway, this guy was nothing I hadn't dealt with before. It was just annoying on a day when I was trying to pay attention to other things.

"Whoa, whoa, whoa, wait a second," Trey's voice came from next to us. I had been catching the combo, so I didn't look at him until after Sam finished.

Trey was looking at Sam with a serious expression. "Are you seriously just going off like that. She's a lady, bro." Trey looked at me. "Has he been going like that the whole time?"

"It's okay," I said.

But the round was over and we were all breaking apart. It was the end of class, and my dad saw that Trey had said something to Sam. Dad diffused the situation by using Sam as an example. He called Sam over and began giving a boxing demonstration, going over a certain combination and explaining why it was effective at close range.

I stood next to Trey while we watched my dad. He glanced at me. "Are you okay?" he asked.

"Yeah, of course," I said. "But it's sweet that you would take up for me."

My dad was saying something to the class, so Trey and I spoke quietly and discreetly.

"I'll go with that guy next time," Trey said, with a serious expression.

I smiled and shook my head at him, and both of us turned to look at my dad. He was demonstrating a counter on Sam, and he did it with an edge of roughness. As a fighter, showing tough physical love was something Dad did all the time. It was a type of conditioning they did around here. He was rough with people he loved in order to toughen them up. He would often slap hard on the back when he hugged people. He knew where to draw the line, however, and Sam didn't. He didn't mean harm, but he was new, and he needed to learn.

Dad told Sam that there was no need to go so hard with our training partners—especially the ladies. He put it in a way that gently but firmly let Sam know he needed to chill out during drills.

Class broke up after Dad's speech, and I stood there talking to Trey while we took off our gloves and pads.

"Does that stuff happen to you all the time?" he asked, looking at me with a concerned but slightly confused expression.

I gave him a reassuring smile. "It's not as bad as it looked or sounded. Those pads are thick. It's more noise than anything. And I know how to meet his punches just right where it hurts him worse than it hurts me. His hands and wrists are probably going to be way more sore than mine."

He shot me that irresistible half smile.

"What?" I said, smiling back.

"You."

"What about me?" I asked, stepping to the side so someone could get past me to the equipment rack.

"You're... uhhh..." he trailed off with a breathy sigh that said he wasn't sure what to say. "I've never known anyone like you, Tara, not even close." He said it quietly and casually, shaking his head as he finished taking off his hand wraps.

"Well, same here," I said. I filtered my response because someone else was walking past us as I spoke.

I smiled regretfully at him since I knew it was a vague thing to say. I just didn't want to say what I was thinking which was, *"I've never met anyone like you either, Trey Harper. I'm in love with you and I want to be with you forever and ever. Please marry me and let's have little Bank Street babies."* No. Instead, I said, "I'm amazed that you're picking all this up so fast."

He smiled. "I had fun."

Chapter 21

The following morning

Trey had to go back to Nashville this morning.

I was not prepared for him to go.

We had seen a lot of each other during the last week, but I couldn't help but feel like some of our time had been wasted. Maybe I was just salty because it was time for Trey to leave and the day had gotten here far too quickly. The last few days had been amazing—the stuff of fairytales. Trey and I looked at each other in a way that said we were in love. We had a connection that had intensified at such a rapid pace that I didn't understand how I was supposed to make it without him.

We ate dinner with my parents and brother last night. My Aunt Abby and a couple of cousins came by while we were there, and Trey charmed all of them. My dad even liked him. He gave him family scoop and said things that I never imagined he would say.

We were at my parents' house until eight, and then we went walking on the beach until midnight.

I felt like Cinderella where everything came crashing down at midnight and I had to go back to the reality that he was leaving.

We got a few hours sleep and then we woke up early and met for breakfast at the diner on the corner.

We were just finishing up, and we knew he needed to get on the road within the next half-hour.

"Do you want to go to the room for a minute?" I asked as we stood up from our place at the table.

There were a lot of people in the diner, but we were right next to each other when we stood up, so I got away with asking the question quietly.

Trey looked at me. His brown eyes were so dark that they appeared bottomless.

"I knew you were going to ask me that," he said.

"You did?" I said, flashing him a smile. "Did you know if you would say 'yes'?" I asked.

"I would never turn you down on that," he said, casually tossing a whopping ten-dollar-bill on the counter as a tip. Our whole meal was barely over ten dollars, and he seemed like a movie star when he just tossed a ten out there, not caring if anyone noticed.

I was lost in thought when Trey took off, so I just followed him. I peered down absentmindedly as I walked. I heard my name. "Tara Castro!"

It wasn't a surprise for me to hear my name since I often saw people I knew at Carson's. I looked up to find Mr. Donnie, a friend of the family—an older guy—my grandpa's age. He was a woodworker who had made furniture for all of us, and I had grown up seeing him and checking in with him over the years.

I stopped at his table even though I was anxious to get to my appointment in the secret room. Mister Donnie would expect me to. Trey came with me. Donnie stood up to give me a hug.

"How are you, Mister Donnie?" I asked, reaching out to hug him.

"I'm fine, Tara, how are you?"

"Good. Doing really well."

"Are you still living across the street?"

"Yes sir. Trey actually owns that building. He's the one who's been fixing it up." I smiled and gestured at Trey standing beside me, but then I kept talking. "I'll be opening up a ballet studio where Mr. McCain was."

"Oh, really? I didn't know that. I knew you used to go over there to Gwendolyn Marshall's all the time for ballet lessons."

"Yes sir, Ms. Gwendolyn's been my teacher for years. She's going to help me with opening this new place."

"Well, that's good," Donnie said.

"Donnie's the one who made that half-circle table in my entryway," I said, turning to Trey.

"Oh, nice, wow, that's a great piece," Trey said, looking at Donnie with a thoughtful expression now that he knew something about him.

Seeing that Trey was impressed, Donnie said, "You're welcome to come by my workshop anytime."

"I'd love to," Trey said. "Maybe I'll get in touch through Tara."

"I'd like that," Donnie said, shaking Trey's hand. "Wh-uh, I'm getting a delivery tomorrow—some teak wood and mahogany—if you want to see how it comes in."

"Oh, thank you for the offer, and I actually really would do that, but I'm headed back to Nashville. I have to leave for the airport in just a minute or two."

"Oh, I see. I didn't realize you weren't from here." Donnie glanced at our hands, which were interlocked.

"Yes sir," Trey said. "I live just south of Nashville. I'm just here part-time, for now."

"Oh, I see," Donnie said.

I reached out and hugged him. "Bye, Mister Donnie," I said.

"Bye, sweetie. Nice meeting you, Tara's friend."

"Nice meeting you, too," Trey said.

He pulled me out of the diner. I saw someone else I knew by the door, and they called to me. I called out a greeting to them, but I didn't stop. Trey was leading me, and he kept walking.

We made our way out of the diner and onto the sidewalk. We crossed Bank Street at the corner and walked up the sidewalk that would take us back to Trey's building and the secret room.

He held my hand as we walked. We said a few things about Donnie, but I was too sad to cope. My heart ached. I wanted him to stay so badly. I was trying to smile and act normal while in the middle of heartbreak feelings.

And then, out of nowhere, Trey pulled me in an unexpected direction. He walked into the hardware store instead of just walking past their door like I anticipated he would do.

"Where are we going?" I asked.

"I need to grab something in here real quick," Trey said.

I almost asked if it was something for his trip, but I decided to stay quiet. I walked alongside him, not saying a word, while he quickly walked through the hardware store. Trey had been in this store several times, and it didn't take him long to find what he was looking for. He came to a section of tools, and let go of my hand long enough to reach out and pick up a giant sledge hammer.

Trey tossed it over his shoulder and began to walk toward the register. I had no idea what was going on. He paid for it, and we left the hardware store with a giant hammer slung over one shoulder. He held onto me with his free hand.

"I assume you're not taking this on the plane with you," I said.

"No," he said.

"What are you doing with it?" I said, finally asking the obvious.

"I'm sorry to do this," he said, in a somewhat regretful tone.

"Do what?"

"I'm not entirely sure," he said.

"When is this happening? Are you doing something right now?"

"I'll see," he said. "Just give me a second."

He walked into the doorway of the Seabreeze Apartments and then climbed the stairs, looking like he was on a mission. I had the feeling he was going to do something crazy. He was pumped-up, and I knew something was going to happen with that hammer, I just didn't know what.

"What's happening?" I asked, as Trey unlocked the door to my apartment.

"I'm going to make sure it's okay. Before I do anything…" He trailed off and walked through my apartment and into my bedroom. He looked intense, moving quickly and easily toting twenty pounds of hammer.

He went into my spare bedroom and walked to the far wall. I was standing several feet behind him and to his left, and there was a mirrored wall to his right. I watched him through his reflection because I could see his face better that way. He walked toward that back wall, staring at it intensely. He reached out and touched a spot on the wall before stepping back and taking a minute to survey the situation.

I had no idea what to think. I just watched him, feeling excited and nervous. He looked at me.

"I'm just going to open this up right here so it—" but he stopped talking in mid-sentence and gave a light swing, denting in a section of the wall.

He must have thought the test was favorable because without warning, he reared back with the hammer and struck the wall with a full, breathtaking swing.

I wasn't in any sort of danger, but I yelped and jumped back because I did not expect him to do that. I knew he had a sledge hammer and I could tell he wasn't messing around, but honestly, I never dreamed he would rear back and rip into the wall like Babe Ruth.

And there he went again, another roaring whack. He swung back smoothly and then hit the wall with a force I was not expecting. That one was so hard that I could see light stream in from the other side of the wall where he had broken through. I gasped and my heart pounded, but I couldn't help but smile as I watched him.

He looked at me. "Sorry, but the next time I come here. I'm staying with you. I'm sorry to make a mess and to do all this at the last minute, but I can't take it anymore. This way, with no wall here, we don't have a choice. I'll have to just marry you before the next time I come. I'll send someone to come make this a proper door or opening, or whatever you decide."

"Are we making this one big apartment," I asked, shocked.

"I figured we would," he said reasonably.

I walked over to him, staring into his eyes. "Then I'll be able to get into the secret room from my apartment," I said.

"That's the idea," he said.

"I guess it'll be our apartment."

"It already is ours. That's what this hole's all about."

"Is it crazy that I love that you just bashed a hole in the wall?"

"Not at all, especially seeing as how this particular wall was just in the way."

"This whole moment, in a weird way, feels a little like a proposal," I said.

"I hope it's not too weird, because it is definitely a proposal. I'm marrying you, Tara. At least I hope so. I want to. If you do."

He paused and looked at me as if waiting for an answer, and I just smiled and said, "Yes."

"Okay, good. Thank you. I'm going to buy a ring and get it to you. I'll mail it if I have to. I'll work it out. I love you, though, Tara, and I'm not letting you go. I don't see why we should spend any more time apart when we know we want to be together. I'd like to have the wedding in Nashville so my people can get to know you, but as far as our living situation, I guess I'll just move here. It seems like the logical choice for us, at least for now. Is that okay?"

"Yes!" I said, smiling and holding back tears.

"I'm also going to send someone to help you make a plan for this apartment. Do whatever we need to do to join the two." He gestured around us. "Think about what you want. You can configure it how you want. I'm sorry I put a hole in your wall. I just wanted to... I hoped that maybe it being here would force us to move things along."

"I should say so," I said, peering through the hole into his apartment. "We're going to have two kitchens."

I glanced at him and he smiled. "Yeah," but as he said it, he turned and grunted and shoved the heavy hammer into the wall. I was standing close to him, and he performed a tight swing so that he wouldn't hit me. But his motion was efficient, and he bashed a significant chunk of the wall out of the way, pushing the pieces so they would fall into his side of the apartment. "Sorry, I had to even it out."

"You're good at that," I said. "I wish you had time to do the whole thing so I could just step through."

"I wish I did, too," he said. "But this will have to do for now." He set the hammer down on the floor next to him. "I'll send someone over to clean it up and make better access." He reached out and took me into his arms as he spoke. "I didn't plan on doing that, I just talked to Donnie about touring his woodshop, and I was all pumped up, so I..."

I laughed at the thought of Donnie pumping Trey up. "You were not pumped about Donnie," I said.

"I was a little. Not so much him, but how you were with him. How you are with everybody. I just see you interact with people, and I feel like…"

He hesitated, and I said, "…like you need to bash holes in walls?"

"Exactly," he said, hugging me. "Just talk to Todd or whoever I send by about the two-kitchen thing. We'll get a designer in here who will know what to do—how to tie the two together. You guys can make a plan."

"Okay," I said, feeling overwhelmed but in an excited way.

"And I guess when Charlotte and Mickey move out, we can take over the back apartment, too," he said. "If you want. Or we can keep it empty and save it for guests. We'll talk about it. We have time."

"I don't care," I said. "I just want the man."

He pulled me in, hugging me, holding me, wrapping his big arms tightly around me. He took a deep breath, and I could feel his lungs expand. I smiled as I leaned against him.

"My head's spinning with all the things I have to take care of and tie up in Nashville. I have so much property over there. I'm probably not even going to start selling it right away. I've got a lot to do and think about." His eyes met mine. "But I'm not doubting it for a second," he added.

"I hope not considering the construction you've already started," I said, gesturing to the hole.

"Which… I'm sorry, mister Harper, but I'm not even sure if you had a permit for any of this."

He laughed and then ducked, kissing my neck and making me squirm and squeal. His smile faded and he regarded me thoughtfully as he pulled back.

"I cannot wait to be with you and not say goodbye again," he said.

"I'm so excited for that, too!" I was genuinely excited, and he smiled at my innocence.

He kissed me, his perfect mouth touching mine. "My girl, Tara, coming to Nashville to get married," he said, teasing me.

I smiled. "And to meet your parents. I'm nervous."

"They're going to love you."

"I love you, too." I said, misunderstanding him on purpose.

He paused for a second, but he knew what I had done. He smiled. "Yeah, well, I love you too, too," he said.

Epilogue

Trey
A year later

Tara absolutely loved that hole in the wall.

She kept it like it was for a couple of months, until construction on 202 had finished and it was time to join the two apartments. The contractors lined the other side with plastic so that she had privacy and so none of the dust from the construction could travel into her side of the apartment.

Tess had fallen in love with the hole the same way her daughter did. Tara told her mom the story of how it happened, and upon seeing the small area of destruction, Tara ran home, grabbed paints, and painted a frame around the hole itself, transforming it into a piece of art.

The plastic on the other side of the hole was blue, and Tess used contrasting colors and painted the frame and the background part of the wall within the frame.

Trey got the biggest kick out of that. He visited Galveston once during the time that it was still up, and he loved what Tess had done. During his visit, they left the barrier in place and Trey stayed on his side of the apartment as they had done in the past.

They didn't get married right away, but they began immediately moving forward with several different plans. They did some work on the pink building, and Trey purchased two other houses in Galveston.

Tara helped him with the deals and some of the property management while he was still tying things up in Nashville. They put off opening the ballet school until January, that way they could get through the construction upstairs and all the noise wouldn't be a nuisance during classes.

They got married in Nashville in December before opening the studio, and that was when Trey finally moved into the apartment. It was huge, and it felt empty without him there during those weeks before their wedding, but Tara had fun setting it up and getting it ready for him.

He was there to stay by Christmas, and it was the greatest relief ever.

That was almost six months ago. The couple passed a winter and spring as newlyweds, getting to know each other in all new ways while being thrown into the whirlwind of moving, buying property, and opening the studio.

They met up in the secret room at least a few times a week, because everyone knew that stolen kisses, secret kisses, were even better than the regular kind.

Trey had hardly come up for air since he met Tara. It was a wonderful whirlwind, but it was indeed a whirlwind.

But after tonight, he would be able to breathe a little easier. He had been anxious, not for himself, but for Tara. Tonight was her studio's first ever dance recital where her students got to show off all that they had learned during the academy's first semester.

Tara was new to being an owner, but she knew it was within her duties to speak to the parents as a whole and make announcements about each group of dancers. She had seen other people run recitals over the years, been a part of many of them, but she was extremely nervous about doing it herself. Tara was nervous, therefore Trey had been nervous.

But now he could breathe easy. In fact, he was breathing better than ever. He was outstanding. The recital had just finished, and Tara had done a perfect job. She had done so well that Trey had no idea why she was anxious in the first place.

She delegated jobs, put together a lovely program, and the dancers and instructors all did great. The whole night was a gigantic success. Trey felt so relieved and excited that he was pumped up as he walked back to the dressing room to meet his wife.

They had both told everyone goodbye after the recital, but Tara went inside while Trey helped her dad and brother load a couple of tables and some chairs into Billy's truck.

"Tara!" he called her name as he went into the dressing room to look for her.

"I'm in here!" she shouted back.

Trey came around the corner and saw her. She looked like she had just stood up. She had her back turned toward him and she was clearing the last few things off of the surface of the vanity in the dressing room.

"Thank you for helping Dad and Will," she said.

Trey caught a glimpse of her in the mirror as she moved to turn off the light, and it looked like she had black streaks running down her face.

"Tara." He said her name in a no-nonsense tone that made her turn to him instantly. "Baby. What happened to you?"

The vanity lights were now out, but there was still plenty of light in the room and he could clearly see that she had been crying. Her cheeks were wet and her makeup was smeared.

She set down the things she had just picked up, two bottles of hairspray and a comb, and turned to hug Trey.

"I'm fine," she said, hugging him gratefully. "I'm just... they're happy tears. Not just happy, but everything. Happiness, relief, just everything. I felt like I was holding my breath going into this, and I was just back here... letting it all out."

He used his finger to tilt up her chin. She was wearing a little black wrap-around dress, and her hair was put up in a neat style, yet there was fresh tears and streaks of makeup running down her face.

She was the most beautiful thing he had ever seen.

"You didn't seem like you were holding your breath," he said.

He held her, crowding her space, leaning her against the counter. She smelled like perfume and sweat. Tara worked hard that night and she smelled like exertion. It was like natural perfume— pheromones. Even her scent called to him. He leaned down and smelled her neck. He kissed her there, and the closeness drove him crazy. He felt desperate to get her home.

"You seemed like you had done it a hundred times," he added. He was so close that she sat on the edge of the counter.

She leaned in and put her arms around his neck. "I don't know what I would do without you. You were the backbone of everything tonight."

"What? No. That was all you."

She let out a little laugh and shook her head. "Oh my gosh, not even close. Everything, Trey. The tickets, the tables, the decorations, the music..." she blinked at him with tears in her eyes. "Even the building where we meet to practice. You gave me this night, Trey. None of this would have happened without you. I need you to know how thankful I am."

Trey smiled at her. "You're welcome," he said, staring into her glossy eyes. "It's cliché to say it's my pleasure, but it actually is."

She gently ran her fingertips down his neck from the bottom of his ear to the top of his shirt collar. She bit the edge of her lip as she did it, regarding him shyly. She was flirting. She knew what she was doing.

"I know, but I just wish there was something I could do to pay you back for everything," she said.

That was it. She knew *exactly* what she was doing. She must not care about that hairspray because it was getting left. Trey ducked and picked Tara up, and she did not protest at all, not even about leaving things in there.

She held onto Trey, snuggling against him, making it easy for him to hold her.

"Thank you, Mister Steve," she said on the way out of the side door of the high school auditorium. "I left a few things in the dressing room, but I'll get them tomorrow when we come back to tear down that backdrop."

"Okay, sweetheart, I'll lock up. Are you okay?"

"Oh, yes sir," she said. "I'm not hurt or anything. He's just carrying me because he wants to."

"And they were happy tears," Trey explained, knowing Steve also saw her smeared makeup.

216

They only got as far as the truck before Trey kissed his wife for what must have been fifteen minutes.

They were parked in a secluded spot near the loading dock, and he couldn't help himself. She was too beautiful to resist. Steve and everyone else were gone from the parking lot by the time they drove through.

They were both insatiable on the way home, too. They kissed every time they had to stop at a traffic light. Tara leaned in and kissed him the first time they caught a red light, and from then on, Trey prayed they would catch more of them.

He knew where they were going and they knew what would happen when they got there. The tension between them was palpable. Tara kept a hold of his arm the whole time he drove. She was shaken with anticipation, relief, and a whole host of emotions.

It was a beautiful, balmy evening in May, but they were only outside for a few seconds, and neither of them will ever remember the weather because they were too busy kissing. The passion and excitement trumped everything else. They kissed as soon as she stepped out of the truck, and it was impossible for either of them to stop, even when they were walking.

There was no telling how they ended up inside the apartment. The trip from the truck to the door was one big passion-filled haze for both of them. They'd break apart and walk a few steps, being playful and smiling, and then they'd kiss again. Finally, they made it to the door. The whole set of apartments was now officially their private house. Charlotte and Mickey moved out when their lease was up, so the whole entryway was now private and kept locked. Tara and Trey considered the stairwell to be part of their house.

Trey locked the front door.

They were gloriously alone.

Tara grinned at her husband after he locked the door, and he gave her a mischievous smile.

She leaned against the railing, tilting her head downward and looking at him like she wanted in on his mischief.

And the rest, as they say, was history.

The End
(till book 5)

Thanks to my team ~ Chris, Coda, Jan, Glenda, and Yvette

Made in the USA
Middletown, DE
20 November 2021